Nochita

Dia Felix

City Lights Books | San Francisco

This book is also available in an e-edition: 978-0-87286-613-3

Library of Congress Cataloging-in-Publication Data
Felix, Dia.
Nochita / Dia Felix.
pages cm.
ISBN 978-0-87286-612-6 (pbk.)
1. Lesbians—Fiction. 2. Bildungsromans, American. 3. Runaway children —Fiction. I. Title.
PS3606.E3883N63 2014
813'.6—dc23

2013040669

City Lights Books are published at the City Lights Bookstore,
261 Columbus Avenue, San Francisco, CA 94133.
www.citylights.com

For Bobby Ray

Nochita

I LOOKED FOR HER everywhere, I never stopped this work. I thought I felt her among the trees at the grove, a little something happened with the light and the dark and the grit in between and I thought her spirit was there, flitting around like an invisible ribbon, but nothing magic happened. Another time I thought her spirit was in a piano, but when I tried to receive her (I put one hand up and one down like the Sufis for correct reception), nothing spoke to me. I cannot pinpoint the exact moment but at some point I got the idea that the place I would find her would be a flat, round object. A flat, round object. I became obsessed with things of this shape, visions of round things sparkled in my skull all the time. The black rubbery rounds of gum on the sidewalk especially. Record albums, plates, even tires caught my eye and reeled me in, I turned up my senses, ready to receive her. Nobody else saw it, and that was fine. I got pretty good at drawing circles by hand, this became a secret meditation. Or I'd trace one, drawing around the bottom of a can for instance, and then I'd take the can away and draw and redraw over the guide, around and around. When I ate tortillas, not joking, she felt close, like she might materialize and outstretch her arms to embrace me. Fold me back in to the place where she lives, lift me into the clouds, above the clouds, to dissolve my body and unbecome like she had. *I'm here*, I'd say. *Take me. Talk to me. Hello? I'm ready, I'm ready, ready now, ready now.*

My heart was always open to her invitation. But that dumb bitch never came. She never appeared out of a tortilla or a saucer to carry me into her balmy afterworld. She stayed away, with her lips sewn tight, she did not rescue me, she remained very thoroughly dead. I was alive and she was not.

One

Awake

WIG PIG EGG RAINBOW scatter dog! Tongue eye jacket of feathers. Raisin morsel drawer open mouth fringe cup palm of grease. Only once has it happened totally totally. I knew I was dreaming because I was in a drugstore kind of like the actual family-owned, dusty-shelved drugstore called Cornette's in our neighborhood, but it wasn't Cornette's and every time I looked away and then looked back the stuff on the shelves had changed. At first there were piles of scarves, then when I looked again they had become shelves full of motorcycle helmets and bowls and then there were bottles of weird lotions and hair stuff and I said *Aha, I know what's going on here, I've been trained!*

So I took control. I magicked myself into a boat. I sailed under a stony gray bridge, and friendly nudging dolphins appeared beside me wearing shiny, rubbery red vests. Also in the boat was a basket with a tiny furry dog in it, smaller than my hand. And there was a lady passing us on a water-bicycle contraption, and I asked her to take off her wig and she did and she was perfectly bald! Then I asked her to take off her clothes and she *did*, and her breasts were lemons! I wanted to be underwater, and next thing I know I'm down there, looking through a curtain of seaweed, able to breathe the water in, the water is thick like frosting and cool like the inside walls of a fridge.

Beautiful, El. Good job. Now, if you can, visualize doing a similar thing, except that you're in everyday waking life. So, you're living life, but you have this knowledge about a world that's more real, a more lucid kind of world. Can you imagine that?

So life becomes a lucid dream?

Does it? I think so. That's illumination, El. That's what we're all after.

Before Kaia had followers, we lived behind the Good Earth Radical Love Food Co-op in a small bedroom behind a curtain, and there were always meetings where people yelled and cried, and the toilet was often broken.

Now we live in our very own cottage at the beach, and we each have a bedroom although I often prefer to sleep under the house.

The Thoughtline

EEEEEP!

Here's a quick tip.

When you're obsessed with all the things that are going wrong, think about the things that are going right.

When you are obsessed with the things that are going wrong, think about softly swaying reeds, shuffling together at dusk.

Every living thing is breathing in its own way. Breathe in your way.

When you are obsessed with how things are going wrong, think about your good body, the infinity of functions performed correctly, wordlessly, striving naturally toward vitality and optimumness, fulfilling its perfect, perfect nature.

When you are obsessed with the things that are going wrong, consider that there is not 'wrong.'

Soften to everything.

WHEN YOU ARE OBSESSED with the things that are going wrong, take a deep three-part breath. Feel the air coming into your bronchial tree, from the silvery tips of the leaves down to the black roots, the kiss of life, the one truth, one life. It is inside you. The beginning of the universe is inside you.

Moment Happening.
Welcome to here.

By Heart

YESTERDAY AT THE BONFIRE at the beach, wood was burning in a big triangle. There was a man tending the fire and someone said that he had it down to a "fine art." Why do grown-ups say these things? "Fine art." And do you know the story "by heart?" You should know your home address "by heart." I kept thinking of the words "fine art" forever in my mind. The fire clapped up into the sky.

Certain things were trying to push through the flames to appear. Things I saw included: the face of the Wizard of Oz from the movie, an ugly white shoe like a mean nurse would wear, a hand saying *stop*.

I FOLLOWED A STRING of seaweed along the beach, I followed and followed until I was far away from the party, it led me to something. It was a seal on the sand, dead, a dark mound, frozen with melted eyes. On its side. Its bottom tail-thing was breaking apart. I screamed and ran back fast.

A lady said, *What did the creature teach you?* And I said, *It showed me sadness*. I felt my heart being pinched in my chest from the sadness of the poor dead thing. I put my face into a towel, I let the heavy feelings go. In my imagination, the seal swam off happily with its family. There were some other kids there who heard me talking about it and wanted to see the dead seal too. I didn't want to show them. They could find it themselves if they need to see a dead seal so bad. Someone became upset because hot wax had spilled onto her new spiritual drum. Someone gave me a pair of their sweatpants to wear when the sun had set and it was cold, they bagged at my ankles. I was tired so I went to rest in the backseat of Little, our orange VW bug. I wanted to dream of riding on the back of seals as they swam, I asked for that dream, I kissed myself.

My Third Eye Is Metal

Tea is made from water that does not boil, but makes an angry sound in the kettle to say that it wants to be removed from the flame. The tea is bright green, sings a green harp song, alien slurp food. Aliens might be real, they might not. You can never know a thing a hundred percent. Some people think they know things but they deceive themselves and they are more limited. Better to just live in mystery. My third eye is a question mark, I feel it coming and going like waves of the ocean. When I slow down I can feel it, the pulsing gray-blue mystery between my eyes like a slow, subtle heartbeat and *so can you*. I can feel my brain whoosh and shine like the purpley inside of a giant seashell. When I *feel into it*. Kaia sips her tea from a round green cup with no handle, a big giant pea, she slurps. Sometimes she lets me have a little bit sweetened with maple syrup, it tastes like electricity plus vitamins, she calls it "kid-crack," and usually I have to beg for it but today I don't need any. Inside my brain are a million giant slides and everyone alive on the earth of all ages is sliding around on them. My heart is in my throat.

Church

My favorite outfit right now is the American flag bikini with the shiny blue cape. My favorite shoes are red rubber cowboy boots. They are technically rainboots but I can wear them when I want to wear them where I want to wear them. With my heels I shoot out magic forces behind me like water from invisible sprinklers. My cape was once a tablecloth, now it's tied around my neck with a string and some safety pins (I'm careful with those). It's fun because it's so light it has no weight.

Now I'm balancing on a plastic chair on a square of mangy red carpet with fraying edges. Chair, square. What. Balancing on one leg. Small chairs for the smaller people. But standing on it I am tall. Kids have wiped boogers and wads of gum under these chairs, kids have puked recently, I feel it. There is a thick smell in the air that reminds you that a lot is going on here. On the subject of smells, the liquor-store lady told me this morning that I smelled like a toilet but she's a judgmental asshole so forget her.

Balancing steady on the chair still, I am tree-trunk straight, a streak of light, a rock, trying not to fall, although I have fallen a number times and it ain't no big deal. Flexibility. I'm a Superhero, no training, born free. Look under the rock. Look under the carpet. Smells like play doh and nasty pee in here is what. Pee smells like honey a little bit. Nasty kids. Sucking on pennies. Now I will stop thinking about things and investigate things.

Under a shelf in the deep dusty darkness I find a shiny black paperback book with soft brown pages and I am moving it up to my nose and then pulling it away, making the glossy red mouth on the cover go in and out of focus.

Oh honey, that's a book for grown-ups! A lady in a pleated skirt snaps the book from my hands. I grab the book back from her witchy clamp. But she holds on tight and I hold on tight and the book floats tensely between us.

It's okay, Kaia softly commands to the woman. *She has a very old soul.*

The witch's face softens. We've blown her mind.

Kaia is bent over, her upside-down face floppy, froggy and very pink. She executes her favorite sequence of postures, a ring of followers do it with her, copying her. They're a ring and she's the diamond in the ring. Circle of silly clown butts, ice cream cones, ears of butt-corn. Ridiculous adults. They close their eyes as they roll their heads around on their necks like it feels so amazingly good. I am a natural animal crawling around, while they have wooden sticks for bones and have to be told what to do. They turn into round eggbabies, roll down a green buttery hill.

Bend over growling like a big mother cat. Root around like a pig. Root, root. A pig has pig nature. A pig obeys only pig law. Breathe tall, breathe wide. Feel your person-nature. Woman-nature. Man-nature. Mothering-nature. Everything about you is right.

Then she puts on the papery white robe with gaping armholes. It makes her look smaller, like a child dressing up in grown-up clothes. People are around her, tending her, she's keeping everyone cool. A coral-colored scarf is wrapped tight around her skull. I don't like that color, it gives me a bad reaction. One neat braid of hair lies against her back like a shining silver fish. One of her followers must've braided it, since when she braids it herself it's so bad that I make her pull it out. There's a blanket of excitement hanging in the air. A woman with a million teeth pins a stiff lily to Kaia's robe, and then pins a tiny microphone beside the flower, her hands moving like hummingbirds.

Hey, don't upstage me with that flower! Kaia jokes, because the flower really is huge! Especially on her small frame. But it's beautiful, cloud-white with perfect flesh, swirling into itself. Oh, I want ice cream!

Are you ready, teacher? the flower pinner asks.

Kaia nods.

We follow the lady into the auditorium like a small parade, I bring up the rear, I'm the caboose. I spin in single revolutions.

HOLY LABORATORY OF THE lord upstage! This church is seriously vast! It rolls in a great wave upward from the stage, and every seat is filled with a human person, and there are people clustered at the back too, covering up the doors, a slippery, twitching sea. I am pretty sure this is the most famous we've ever been. Everyone is holding their breath, gummy quiet, giving me the squirmies, tappydancies. I do a down dog, visualize a hot air balloon tied to my body pulling my buttbone up with a string. If I had a tail it would be sticking right up. Now I am a thatched roof, a pyramid. Kaia's face bobs around on a huge screen, settling in—a billboard-sized video projection, a live feed so everyone can see her face as big as a house, even those pinched in the way way back. Little eyebrows, shiny pink skin, eyes *like open windows.*

Eyes, windows open. Heart, guiding lantern. Swing, gently, swing.

I can see the individual hairs of her eyebrows on the screen, the tiny black dots on her nose. It gets quiet, then the stir of applause.

No. No applause, Kaia says, gently holding up one hand like 'stop.' *We don't need to fill up the space around us. Can you see how it's already perfectly full? Those seconds moving past us.* Her onstage voice is darker, deeper than her mom voice and there's a little whistle when she makes an S. I am considering eating my boogers.

I can hardly see you all! These lights are bright up here . . . they're videotaping today. I'm a cel-eb-rit-ee. I think I like it.

Is everybody breathing?

The crowd happy-sighs, jelly balls, hands on bellies, plastered smiles. Totality, bliss bestowed, easy peasy.

To be fully present is easy to say and—easy to do. We are doing it now—together. This is it, kids, life. Mine, yours. Ours. What do we think? What is the sensation? Can we call it something? Could we call it—love?

Could we call it—family?

Can we live, for one moment, together, in a state of non-effort?

She puts her hands up like a mime against an invisible wall. Then puts her palms together like prayer. Some people in the audience copy her. Silence falls like feathers, like floaty fibers of dandelions, the vibe is crackly sacred, getting quieter, something sinking

Kaia squints into the audience.

In the black coat, I see you. I remember you. Aren't you hot in that?! And you, you came to my last talk, right? In Los Angeles? Yes, I thought so. I remember you. I can barely see you though.

When she talks to someone they flush pink and then glow like a candle.

Those who read my last book, Moment Happening, *know that I've been hovering around this idea of the adult child. The truth of that. Of living that. Moving toward that freedom. I go where my heart leads me. My heart is my calculator. My heart leads me like a dog on a leash. I think I'm walking the dog, but then every once in a while I look down and say, goodness! This little dog is walking me!*

Everyone's a beginner. Here's something silly, I bought myself a child's tea set at the Goodwill. The kind I had always wanted when I was a girl. I made tea in the little pot, black tea actually, and sweetened it with honey, and had tea with myself, sitting on the floor. I drank ten cups of tea, each cup held a few tablespoons. I really did this. Meanwhile, my seven-year-old is in the corner reading Camus.

A bit of laughter.

I'm kidding of course. She was reading Nietzsche.

Ha ha ha ha. This is kind of my cue, I feel.

I crawl in front of her, across the stage, to the darker side where a cluster of plants in giant clay pots loom unlit, where a basket of crayons and paper have been set out for me, and a meditation cushion. It's a jungle! Tiny wild pigs, spiderwebs, spiny stalks. I gnaw from a milky root to survive for days, use those good teeth. My favorite animal is the parrot. Marie Curie's favorite animal was a shark. I am feeling like an actual elephant. The dirt in the plant pots is dark and wet and smells of vitamins, magical tinyturds. I lick my finger and use it to pick up some black dirt and then drop it back, so now I am part of the plant, my particular chemicals.

My daughter. She is happiness. She is my best teacher.

Looking at me. I shake my butt a little.

We are born knowing how to live and then we forget. Diderot said, 'you all die at fifteen.' He was talking about women, and for us it's especially true, but it's true for everyone. Let's help each other remember how to live. To live fully.

She's looking at me still. They're all looking at me, they want to be delighted by me, the teacher-child. So I produce a magical blue fart cloud from my butt. I unscrew the lightbulbs with my mind and send them floating like a gang of ghosts toward the back doors. I feel the sharks inside my head, nudging their noses to get out. I drift out the window in a gravity-free bubble. I roll around, making a little show, a bug clawing at the air, cracking crayons under my back. If I grab my private area, they will laugh more, ha ha ha ha. I should not destroy crayons though, I should be respectful of the good crayons, they are so decent. My spine is stronger than a crayon spine.

Now I will copy a picture from the grown-up paperback book I found, with the shiny lady's lips on the cover. I'm good at *rendering*, I was an artist from the moment I came into this world, we are all artists, yes, but some of us are very in touch with our gifts and I am one of these lucky ducks. There are drawings inside the grown-up book and in one of them, a man is doing something between a woman's legs and the woman is happy, she has dark puffy hair like Wonder Woman and a big smile, a laughing smile. Even with crayons I can do good pictures but I prefer pencils.

You, in pink.

A pale woman with big brown glasses rises and bounces down toward the stage, her hand patting her chest.

Come oooonnn doowwn! The price is right!, I say.

So wonderful to meet you, teacher!, the woman says, clasping Kaia's hand. *I've read all your books. I feel like I know you. When I read*

Moment Happening, *I had a feeling that you were writing the book directly to me. It was like a beam of light shining into the darkest corners of my depression. You helped me heal. I got off medication, I planted a garden . . . finally got rid of my husband's stuff . . . ex-husband . . . I had been divorced almost three years and his sweaters were still hanging there in the hall closet . . . I just could not accept . . . oh god, I can't believe I'm one of these people up here crying. This is exactly what I wasn't going to do!*

Yes, says Kaia. *Everyone, do you see her crying? Of course you mustn't credit me for healing you. Healing happens inside. But then you knew I would say that.*

The woman sobs now, then blows her nose right into the microphone. She tries to stop crying because she wants to talk more but she sobs and sobs and fans her face, and some people in the audience are laughing. Not cruel laughing, merry laughing, everyone loves everyone!

I PUSH OPEN THE heavy door and tumble into the warm stale sun. Squares of new glittery peachy concrete roll out forever, a sparkling desert. I touch every corner with the toes of my boots. Everyone is inside, so this church courtyard area is deserted. Commence my flying exercises.

I feel something coming into my bones, a low rumbling, what is the message? I get so quiet, I can hear my own heartbeat. A tribe of skateboarders drops from glass branches, ghost monkeys attacking the air with shooting and scraping, flying whizzing planks, shouts and grunts, bad words, globs of spit. Their ape hands hang low. I put up my energy shield.

Cool outfit!, one of the boys says to me.

Are you a superhero? asks another.

A sore on his face, freckles. I know they could take me or kill me, and this excites me in some of my chakras (like driving fast down a hill), but they shoot right through me, they don't touch me. I listen closely until their roar fades into nothing, until I hear just the shifting of leaves on the giant tree like papery coins, and the happy spitty splatter of the fountain. I relax under the shady tree until sound is a chandelier, the bright sun a grid of twisting snails under my eyelids.

Well, it's not easy to take off the cowboy boots because I'm not wearing socks and they rubberly stick to my baby sasquatch feets. Ultimately I do eeek them off and walk into the fountain, lady of diamonds, diamonds dripping from my fingers. Water comes to my knees. Cool glass. I am careful because it's very slippery, it's not made for people to go in, I remember that from last time we were here. There are coins in the fountain, including quarters, and I leave them alone, I make that decision. I have to pee and I do not pee in the fountain, I make that decision. I will pee into the toilet standing up, I am getting good at that, so much better, I don't get pee on my legs or all over the place, but even if I do, pee is sterile. I remember this from when we lived at the Good Earth Radical Love Food Co-op and there was a big deal made when a man tended to pee in the kitchen sink and that was what he said to defend his behavior, that it was sterile. He was actually cleaning the sink by peeing in it, he said.

I love the bathroom at this church so much because there is a bed in it. The wallpaper, which I also really love so much, is shiny silver with yellow drawings of a fist holding flowers printed over and over forever. In the bathroom mirror there is one me—finger coils of dark hair, light brown skin, poochum tummy, strong legs, the monkey feet, coffee bean eyes. I take off my bikini top by pulling the string back there, reveal! Chocolate chip nipples! Baby shrimpy toes. Adults have horrible smashed wreckage toes, thick sticks for toenails. My toes will never look ugly like that, I vow. I vow today. I make a decision. I do all kinds of poses—elegance, strength, mystery. Elephants are always naked.

I put up my shield, two crossed fists, up! *Ready!*

My name is Ele-phant! My name is Ele-phunky! My name is hunky hunky!

There is a thin green bedspread covering the bed very tidily. I wonder if anyone ever died here, or had a baby? Must be. I lie down on it and cover up with my cape. Act sleepy.

Dream of what? I'd like to go to the moon this time, break off a little chunk, taste it. It would taste like sweet-tarts. This is what I try for, but the skateboarding boys swill back to mind without invitation, their big floppy shoes with holes, rough elbows, animal haircuts. Dangerous. Then another dream chapter, Kaia's in a white bikini, sunbathing on a rectangle of silver foil. Grass surrounds her infinitely in all directions. It feels like a memory, something from real life. From before me, maybe. She does like to sunbathe, or she used to, slathering up her skin with coconut oil until it gleams like jewelry. The pursuit of beauty is ancient and natural and does not mean that a person is vain, just as a person who seeks good health is not vain because health and beauty are in fact two sides of one coin! And the sun is not as bad for you as everyone says, it gives you vitamins, it gives everything life! The sun is not the enemy. There is no enemy. The sun is not a source of alternative energy it is the only energy, it makes green things green, it makes everything go. The sun made me. When I sucked on my mother I was sucking on the sun, the sun is my blood. . . .

Kaia's talk is over and the courtyard bounces quickly to life. The happy followers buy books, get in line to get them signed by the Guru, sip from paper cups of blessed herbal tisane. It does not matter if your teeth are not white, if your pearls are fake, if your car broke because you did not change the oil or if you have a wart on your finger. You are exactly perfect, Kaia says so, *in spite of the imperfections your mind may allege*, and today the smiles are real, and for everyone. Still naked except for my cape. I go back into the fountain and I think somebody might stop me but nobody stops me, and someone takes pictures.

The Total Book

HERE'S HOW WE'RE GOING to start, we think, the Total Book of Totality Coloring Book for Kids, Adults, and Everyone Else:

Every breath is a brand-new world.
If we aspire to totality, we aspire to know this, to live this.

I illustrated the layers of consciousness as layers in a cake. She'd asked for a universal metaphor, as this kind of information should not only be for the erudite pathsniffers. So far there is the layer of 'everyday living,' 'pleasure, as in love of cake and ice cream and trashy magazines,' and 'the unembraceable: fear, disease, decay.'

Somewhere in the book Kaia wants:
Scientists may not like my language, but they know what I mean.
Everything is the first thing, the only thing, the last thing, and the same thing.
Everyone is twins.
I am content to be my own living proof.
Personal truth is the Truest.
You are the scientist.

I'm planning to draw the scientist with seagulls flapping around his head, and the ocean wrapping around his feet like a blanket. His heart may be outside of his body, may be up among the clouds, may be hybridized with a car engine, although I don't know how to draw that. Personal truth is the COOLEST. Maybe I will just draw a pair of glasses, but that wouldn't be much fun to color. Maybe a bunch of glasses all smashed together in a swarm. Or big glasses with a magic castle painted over the lenses.

Anyone can wake up to total happiness. It belongs to you and every person from birth. It is our priceless inheritance.

Come on! You can do it! Exercise your birthrights, brothers and sisters! Enemies and darlings!

Flame

I'm sleepy and feel like a baby and I want her to tell me my favorite story, the near-death experience. I put myself under the blanket on the couch, and she obliges, because she can say yes or no and she says usually yes.

You had the prettiest, shiniest head of black hair. You were a dear little friend, a little squirmy piglet, so teeny! So alive! Already you knew how to live, you were born an expert live-er. You said HI! to everyone and everything, to cops, traffic lights, coffee cups. You were born with your heart wide open, grateful, delighted, in love with life. You're still that way, right? The cruel world hasn't beaten it out of you yet, has it?

I open my rib cage and show her my shiny golden heart, turning slowly like a chicken on a rotisserie. She is touching my head with her fingernails, playing with my curls, making tiny circles that hypnotize me into eyes-closed.

It was at night, correct? I want to get to the good part. I arrange the blanket so it covers both of our feet now.

Yes, she says, *it was. It was the very first night you slept outside our bed, in your own little crib. Your father had put your crib in the living room because it was warmer there, it's where the heater vent was.*

Was that the same year it snowed on the Hollywood sign?

No no, that's another story. That happened when I was a kid. This was in the mobile home park right above the beach, in Capistrano.

Capistrano. That's my favorite word. She continues,

But it was a chilly evening. And it was strange lying down without you next to me, not hearing your little breaths, it felt wrong. I couldn't sleep, couldn't even get close to sleep, I kept getting up to check on you. You were fine every time, wrapped up in your blankie, peacefully sleeping. Finally I relaxed and slept a little, and I dreamt—I still remember this dream—that I was in the woods, lost, and a family of big angry bears were there, dancing a spooky dance, jumping and shaking the earth. I woke up scared, and the real world was shaking, shaking for real! The bed was hopping around, the pictures on the walls were swinging. The whole world was completely out of control. I've never known such terror. I lunged out of bed, leapt to the living room to find you. Our mobile home was tiny, a shoebox, but it took an eternity to get to you. All my books had fallen from the shelf and I'm kicking them out of the way and finally I get to the living room and there are little blue flames along the bottom of the wall. Your crib is gone. Gone. The absence of your crib, that empty space . . . the fear . . . I can't even put it into words, it was animal-fear. You'd disappeared. I pat around, the kitchen table is a little bit on fire, on the bottom. Your crib is next to it, finally I see it, it's on fire too, fingers of flames creeping up the legs. I pulled you up and out, your body was still and cool, your little teeny torso, you were so small, just <u>*this*</u> *big.*

She makes a shape with her hands, her fingers all touching.

I ran with you outside, so I could see you under the streetlights—

You're not supposed to go outside in an earthquake!, I say.

Well, I was panicked. I thought you were gone.

Dead!?

Yes, I was afraid. I was just about to scream, I had this lungful of air to scream, when your eyes popped open, your shoulder kind of twitched and you just said, HI!

I was okay!!

You were completely fine! You had slept through the whole thing! You weren't even scared. You were happy . . . like you were always happy when you woke up.

Did my dad put out the fire?

He did.

She likes telling this story usually but this time she seems kind of freaked out. She is sitting up so straight so I smush my face into her warm beachy neck, to show her how alive I am, how much we are fine now.

Connection Comics

Everything in the world is made of the same thing.

When you hurt someone you are hurting yourself.

So be nice to others and to yourself.

One man comes upon a large rock in the woods and sees a rock. Another man comes upon the rock and knows an ancient connection with that rock and sees, and feels his own heartbeat pulsing inside the rock too.

Matter matters.

Our hearts have eyes. Do not put dark sunglasses on your heart's eyes!

When you die it is like changing your clothes. When you die it is like changing your panties.

Everything has hands.

Underworld

IT'S WET DOWN HERE and smells of slugs and mushrooms. It's early and cold but the surfers are already arriving, I can hear them opening and shutting car doors, untying surfboards, changing into wetsuits. They are my alarm clock. Something weird's in my mouth, I chuck it out, it's a piece of gum all hard now. My hair is damp, heavy sandy clumplocks, sand sticks to one side of my face. I get up, rinse off with the hose at soft pressure, closing one eye then the other. I wash my mouth. The water is so cold but I can deal with it. I enjoy goosebumps. I shake my head like a dog. The sky is fresh, ripped-open gray. I like this part of morning, new and minty, before everything. I am tender. My fingers are cold, my belly is empty. When I was littler I remember I filled my mouth with sand as an experiment, and it was a bummer. Our small front yard is all dried up, but it has some fun things in it like two shiny red mushrooms, a flamingo, a gnome, and two yellow-and-orange pinwheels stuck in crooked and turning around mellow-style. I'm cold!

Once upon a time we had a real door, I remember it. Green glass, smeared as if by fingertips, so the outside world looked like a crazy watercolor version of itself. Cars smeared by. Dogs, joggers, homeless guys with shopping carts smeared greenly by. It got broken and now we have a screen door that doesn't lock, and then a beaded curtain with a big red heart beaded into it. I walk through this curtain, entering the house with arms out in front of me like a mummy, strings of wooden beads clacking together behind me. Kaia is up, in the kitchen, pouring dark green slime from the blender into a tall glass. She has the blender all the way upside down but there is still slime in it so she bang, bang, bangs it out. I turn on the electric heater and crouch beside it.

Slept under the house?

Perhaps, I say, chattering.

Rich dreams. Gift of dreams. You like it down there, close to the earth. Her warm hand on my shoulder, squeezing me toward her. She kisses me on the hair.

I don't like you to sleep with wet hair.

I just got it wet!

She takes a big drink of her green slime, it leaves a mossy moustache.

Superb superslime?

Super good, she says. *Want some?*

Barfo.

Want some hijiki? She holds the plate out to me, a pile of black quivering worms which smell like deep-sea.

Barfsville.

What I want is sugar (always). I put on my flipflops and Kaia's giant white sweater and go to the liquor store, where I settle on the semi-usual, a king-size bag of peanut M&Ms and a roll of Smarties.

Bath day today? says the liquor store lady, seething with black hair, but then she gives me a Dumdum for free. She is an unenlightened being always saying some shit.

I love YOU!, I chirp as I leave. I want to fart for punctuation but it doesn't come out, I might poop.

In the Pines

THE SUN IS A blazing orange fist hovering, magnetized over the ocean. A circle of women is moving inside another circle of women, a slow dance where each woman looks into the other woman's face and says, *yes I see you, yes I love you*, then steps over and says it to the next woman in the line until everyone has said it to everyone. One woman has braces even though she is old.

I don't want to do it and I don't have to, I can say no.

I walk into the woods instead, it's instantly darker and cooler under the old tall pines. I don't know anything about trees like the name of a tree but these are obviously pines. Dirt gets inside my jelly shoes, slowing me down. (*When something is not going well, say Hello, and then ask, What are you trying to teach me? Soften to everything.*) The dirt feels good in my shoes, actually.

I find a big smooth rock and sit on it like a million other people have. The ocean is softly crashing. Over and over it falls. The forest is sweet, perfumed, dusty. Dry doves collect and scatter peacefully in the sky, the scene relaxes my skeleton.

Recently I found his old driver's license. My dad's. He did not look particularly handsome or ugly to me, just a macho guy with a thick crown of black hair and a cop-like mustache. But Kaia tells me that he was breathtaking, like a hush fell over a room when he entered. Kaia understood the thing *tall dark and handsome* when she saw my father.

That's where you get your height, says Kaia.

I picture him in an orchard, on a ladder, picking oranges. I want to see his face. I move in, but all I can conjure is the hovering cutout of his thick inky black hair and moustache, paper cutouts composited onto an empty brown face. He offers an orange out to me, wobbly.

I see her before she sees me, her silky sleeves swimming around her knobby wrists as she appears between the trees, wearing the universe's ugliest sandals. She sits beside me.

Found you, she says.

You give me such a full heart, she says. She squeezes my head into her neck, a clumsy hug. *Don't you?* she says.

Roberta

With her shirt untucked I can see the beginnings of Roberta's soft belly, and the blurry darkness of the tattoo under her belly button. It's a bull's head, tilted down angrily with eyes looking up hard, bubbly clouds blowing from his nose. The horns represent Roberta's fallopians, but we mustn't call them fallopians because that's the name given to them by some man who claims to have discovered them, the same infantile patriarchal possessive spirit in which Columbus 'discovered' America, which we should also call something else, and California too. Roberta also has twin snakes coiled around each ankle, hissing at each other at the back, and a few more decorations, and always many silver earrings hanging from both ears and bells on her sandals, as she is a 'funky fairy.' She always wants to 'connect' with me but I don't always want to 'connect' with her. She does not smile. She wants me to finish the Gandhi comic I started so they can put it in the new book in the section called 'change your mind change your life.' If I finish it I'll get paid five hundred bucks but I don't know if I will finish, we'll see. Five hundred bucks, that's a very fancy bike (beach cruiser) and many many very fancy beads made of real crystal, but still I don't know. I am not feeling that *connected* to Gandhi like I was before.

Roberta sets down a thick pile of papers, the latest manuscript.

Wow, says Kaia. *That's a whole lotta words.*

It's pretty much verbatim from your talks, Roberta says. *I just tried to give it some structure.*

Roberta peels an orange like a machine, one long peel is produced which I reassemble back into the orange shape and then smash it with my fist. Kaia is leafing through the pages of her manuscript, she is feeling shy about all this. Roberta inserts film into her camera, they need a new photo of Kaia for press.

Maybe it's better if your Gandhi comic isn't in the book anyway, Roberta says. *Cos Gandhi was a little bit of a misogynist. I mean, that doesn't lessen the coolness of his accomplishments or anything. And I'm totally sensitive to the cultural context. I'm just saying.*

Kaia wants me in the photo but Roberta says no. Sometimes we need to *concede to convention.* She positions Kaia on the couch and fixes her clothes. Kaia does her guru face, her small mouth in an impish smile, her eyes intense, her chin a little bit down. Roberta holds the camera up to her face then pulls it down again and looks at Kaia with her naked eye and some serious vibrations.

What? Kaia says through her smile. *Take the picture.*

You're getting smaller, aren't you? Roberta says. *You've lost more weight, haven't you?*

Daughter

Nochita? This is Jorge. Your father.

My name is Ele-phant now, I say. *Ele-fizz. Ele-Menno. Penumbra Ele-phickle, Funkster.*

This is Nochita? Or, no?

My name is Ele-phant, I say. *Phunky Viva! Shakti Pat! My name is Elephant.*

Your name is 'elephant'? We named you Nochita, did you know that?

Yes, of course I know that! I changed it. A long time ago. I'm kind of being weird right now.

Okay. I . . .

Hello?

Hello? This is your father.

Yes, I get it. I understand.

Good. Listen, I know you're only ten, but I want to tell you something.

I'm eleven.

That's what I said. (He laughs.) *Nochita . . . okay if I just call you Nochita for now?*

Yes, no prob. Can I call you Jorge?

Yes, no problem.

Cool. Are you smoking?

Yes. I'm putting it out right now. It's out. Nochita, I need to apologize to you. I'm an alcoholic. I'm in recovery now. I have to—I want to apologize to the people I've hurt.

Okay, I say.

Okay. Nochita, I'm sorry I haven't been in better touch. I've been in a lot of difficult situations. I've had a lot of troubles. Life has been difficult. But that is not an excuse.

Life is not difficult, I say. *The war is over if you want it. I know the Prince of the Cool-Cave.*

Who?

Good Prince Arjuna. In my heart cave, he bangs the drum.

Okay. Well, people have different experiences. But I'm sorry. That's what I want to say. I'm sorry I haven't been in contact. I'm going to be in better touch from now on. If you will—if you want that. Okay? Hello?

That sounds good, I say. *Are you smoking?*

Yeah, I lit another one, he says. *I know, I shouldn't.*

Why not? I say.

I don't fucking know! he says, and laughs again, I think?

The Thoughtline II

EEEEP!

Well my darlings? I am not feeling well as some of you already know. Amazing how bad news travels! I wasn't going to talk about it but I can't do that heavy gag trip. You understand. We've all spent too much time being gagged, haven't we, girls?

(Clink—the sound of putting a glass of water on a glass table. And ahhh after she swallows.)

Why did I get sick? There's a question! I'd like to know the answer myself! But questions don't always have answers.

I am continuing the work. Focusing on the fundamentals, total acceptance, totality of consciousness, the journey as destination.

But I have also been sleeping.

Please know that your letters and thoughts have been very dear to me—they always are but especially now, in this stranger time. I send love and compassion to you. I may not be as communicative as normal, but please know I still love you. I will not be doing public appearances for now, but you can expect my next book to be available in May as planned.

(A faint sound like something rolling.)

Oh, did you hear that? That little rumble? That's my daughter's sewing machine. She's a slice of the divine, that little one. Not so little anymore! Almost as big as me now! She's making me a placemat, hoping it will make me want to eat. That girl.

Alright, here I go, I'm going now. Lots of love out, and lots coming in. Stay soft my friends.

Click.

A Comet

Kaia opens an envelope from the mail and removes a slender emerald green feather. She admires it, spinning it in her fingers, then tapes it to the wall. All along the wall, in a single wavering line, are little things people have sent us—notes, cards, stones, sticks of incense, drawings, bits of string and fabric and leaves from all over the world. There are also Kaia's own tidy drawings of sailboats, cactuses, doves, her teacup, a bicycle, a bridge. She stands back and looks at the feather.

It's definite now that she has shrunk. I've gotten bigger, like she claims, maybe, but she's gotten smaller, withering like a flower in the heat. There is no longer doubt.

I am opening and closing the cupboards, wanting something to eat besides dried fruit or seaweed or coconut flakes or the hard-boiled eggs that Roberta brings. I find some almonds and eat them, they're chewy and hard, maybe they're from before I was born.

Kaia reclines on the white couch with papers around her legs. Her hand over her mouth like she is thinking about barfing but then her face as calm as stone, eyes closed.

She takes the tape recorder from the coffee table, holds it in front of her mouth, presses the record button.

A floating leaf is mooooooving down the river, she says. *Whose is the hand that moves the leaf?*

She laughs.

No, seriously, I'm asking you!, she says into the recorder. *Whoooooose fucking hand moves the fucking leaf?*

She laughs, not in a nice way but like she is making fun of it, like she is being mean.

Kaia, stop it! I say. *Erase it! Start over! Don't make me come pull your hair! You can't say fuck on the thoughtline!*

What's happening is Kaia doesn't want to do another thought-line but she needs to do one every couple days or people will freak out and come look in our windows, at least this is what Roberta claims.

Eeeeep!

A floating leaf is moving down the river. Whose is the hand that moves the leaf? Friends, I choose surrender. I do, I deeply do. I choose to see that on the fiery ocean of chaos there is an island of peace . . . I will swim to that island, and know that everything I need is inside me right now. I can choose to dwell on that island of real safety. We can choose to dwell on that island. Or we can tread water around the island, we can live in a state of anxiety and unrest. It's my choice. It's our choice.

The late afternoon pours in sun like an egg yolk, the wood floor gleams, the house heats up like the inside of a plastic bag. Kaia and I both have a film of glossy sweat on our upper lips, on the back of our necks. The air is like the inside of a balloon. I open the sticky windows, greeting the families of dead flies. A balmy breeze, the smell of grass baking and the warm salts of the sea move gently through the air, cooling and drying my skin. I put my tongue on my arm and taste the salt.

She is sleeping now on the couch and I lie down on the floor beside her. A strong desire to break things, to throw glasses and plates, arises strangely in my body, a flaming comet. I want to throw the blender out the window, sending all the neighborhood cats running. Rip the lights from the ceiling with one fierce swipe, thrash over the fridge, bite the knobs off the drawers.

Hello, unwelcome and useless impulse. What are you trying to teach me?

I take good breaths until it's gone.

Meditation Hour

I CORRECT HER PONYTAIL. She rolls her butt around the crunchy round pillow to find the correct position for meditation. She's so light she hardly makes an impression.

Sit with me, teacher, she says.

I will, but only for a moment. I am feeling the burning comet feeling again and I want to run out of the house and keep running for hours. Or stomp the glass coffee table and shatter it and shoot beams of blood out of my fingers. I want to run off the cliffs and just keep running in the air, over the ocean, and never drop.

Everything is inside me.

I sit across from her on my knees, I scrape tiny fibers of dead skin from around her raw pink nostrils with my thumbnail. The flesh that became my flesh. The meat that built my meat.

She grabs my wrist suddenly, like swatting a fly.

You must not be afraid, she says, looking deeply into me with fierce eyes, like a bird pecking something.

I'm not afraid. The words roll out of me involuntarily like gas bubbles. She has become a wolf, a skinny wolf, her mouth has a new smell, a new darkness around her teeth.

Okay, she says, removing her cool clamp from my wrist.

She resettles into her tall posture. She closes her eyes and takes a few long breaths. Then she snaps back, again opening her eyes, puts her palm against my shoulder.

You came to me from the center of the earth, you boiled up like lava. The earth coughed and you appeared, still covered in ectoplasm, defenseless, still all folded up. I was entrusted with your care. You were my baby, but you are a daughter of the universe. It has been my honor. Hear me.

I did hear you, I say.

I want you to say, I am a daughter of the universe.

I am a daughter of the universe, I say dully.

It has been my honor, she says. She is freaking me out. She has the ninja energy all of a sudden.

It has been my honor. Your honor.

I HAVE BEEN SLEEPING lately in Kaia's bed, mostly. Sometimes my body lifts straight up like a balloon is pulling me. Sometimes I sink down. Sometimes I rock as if swinging in a giant, slow hammock. I don't think I am really sleeping, only softly resting, like I am one of the pillows on the bed.

I AM FREE-FLOATING IN the sea, free of will, emotion, or direction. Dipping below the surface and exploring the salty gurgling darkness for as long as my breath will allow before emerging, popping up like a ball, seeing the world come back into focus, the salt stinging my eyes. I'm not looking for anything. Certain things touch my body and I don't know what they are, could be jellyfish, kelp, the natural boogers of the deep—or darker things, sniffy sharks, pirates' swords, chunks of ship, inert hand or elbow.

I FIND KAIA ON her meditation cushion slumped against the wall, her soft face smashed into it like a drunk person's. Her mouth is open, her bottom lip wet and shining. I unstick her from the wall, tap her mouth shut, it falls back open. I put my arms around her shoulders, lift her to standing and guide her to the couch awkwardly, two children dancing.

I fell asleep meditating, she says.

Yup. I pat the white blanket around her shoulders. *Now you're comfy*.

You smell like the sea. . . .

She's going to say something else but then she is asleep.

She's suddenly old, her small face exhausted and withered.

I know she's alive because I can see her chest moving and hear the velvety breath from her throat.

Stay alive. Do that one small thing.

Dark Treacle

Not my imagination—THE imagination.
Not my sadness—THE sadness.
Not my struggle—THE struggle.
Not my illness—THE illness.

Don't you feel better?

Vital kundalini energy, swirling watery blood inside pulsing cell shapes, shower of kidney beans and rocks of salt, blurring flowery wallpaper, hands changing into feet, bones growing quickly on trees. Our house is crushed by a fast heavy force, like a big man crushing an aluminum can under his boot. The world is toppled, the world is fresh soil.

I wake up not breathing and have to remind myself to breathe, like turning the ignition on a car.

Imagination is a gift. Thoughts are things.
Deathless. Sadless. Selfless.
THE sad.

The pictures come whether I want them or not. Veins rotting underground, opened up, black oily liquid discharged, thick but fast, splashed in great slashes and dripping down our wet walls. Dead tree branches ooze brown sap from sharp pointy tips. Very knife sharp. A knife cuts open the world like skin. The world doesn't care, or the world shrieks and recoils.

The Cliffs

I UNTACK MY HANDS from her skull. I release her skull from my hands.

The wooden beads make their sweet clacking sound as I breeze through our doorway. In the outside world, reality is held intact by a thin floss netting, the sky is soft like lint, the trees fake, stage trees, a Hollywood Halloween gesture. This world-screen is held intact because someone's pointing a gun at it. It's flimsy, fabric, it could crash right down anytime. She asked me to leave the house and I agreed, I have left. A car drives by, I hear thin music slipping from its windows. There is our car, our little Little, which hasn't been driven in weeks. That was our car. This was our house.

You love and accept me.

The air is polished clean, glassy, cool, a wet rock. Down the hill and along the edge of steep chunky cliffs of reddish dirt with iceplant here and there hanging like trembling fingers over the sea. It's a long long way down there. You're not supposed to walk here but I can. A coil turns slowly under the ocean, white wavelets frozen and buzzing. The water is green today, intense dark emerald with milky stripes. No way am I jumping in it. My flexed feet will not hit and shatter that buzzing wall. I've heard you break when you hit, that it's gross. I've heard that you drown, unable to move, your broken bones a tangled knot, choking you like a scarf. Nope not doing that.

Everyone writes their own book, absolutely.

I take the hairy path down to the beach. Soft lumps of turf sink and sigh beneath each of my steps, a living gesture of welcome.

Scruffy man with disintegrating beard, shoes untied, clutching brown bag. 'Salt and pepper' hair. Pair of jogging women with golden ponytails bouncing in unison, identical red baseball hats. Frowning woman holding one shoulder higher than the other, hunched, tapping and pulling her elbow skin, lips grumbling.

THERE ARE CAVES ALONG the beach, into the cliffs. A few of them are easy to find and tourists like to walk a few feet into them, take a piss or change clothes or leave their candy wrappers or smoochy poochy. But many are hidden and you have to know where they are. Locals only. If you don't surf, don't start.

FIND THE MYTH. FIND the bone cave in the cliff, enter it with your hands. Make a home deep in that bone cave. Will there be a bone-booth? A closet made of bones? Bone hangers, bone shoes. A bone burger. Bone guitar to play. Bone books to read. I'll just curl up in there. Find an outlet for my bone hair dryer. I'll tap out the code and the cliff walls will clank dustily open and I will go in and they will close behind me and I will enter the fold and I will un-become. No more night, no more day. No more air. No more sad. No more nothing.

Learn to trust yourself. Be a nice place for a gaze to fall. Let your heart shine out like a lantern. Let your heart be your compass. Let it show. Let it flow from your fingertips. Let your heart be your compass.

Know that you are a child of god.

Let your eyes be your disguise. Let your stomach be your swimming pool. Let your fists be your guns. Let your skull be a rock, let your teeth be fossils, let your spit be your stench. Let your eyes be fat angry snakes.

Stabbing myself with calming platitudes fails. It's getting darker, the end of the day is coming. I want to disappear but my body keeps existing and my legs keep walking. Wounds do not spontaneously burst from my body. I am just a person who keeps walking. Beyond the cliffs, where the beach opens up, toward the dog-mouth underbelly of the pier, it's always nighttime under the pier. Clouds of frying seafood aroma drift down from the foodstand. Music too, live guitar through a dirty amplifier. Someone's dad's band.

My calves hurt from walking in the sand. I stop and pat out a little ditch for my butt and a little hill for my skull, chucking away the bigger sticks of wood and newer cigarette butts, smoothing it out into my custom bed. I dig my hands into the cool sand underneath. In the water surfers float like soap bubbles, talking without sound, slowly spinning. Up on the pier are fishermen with their buckets and toolboxes, and families strolling, a man with a red balloon tied to his wheelchair moves along. I want to sleep, but I am rubbed-open. She asked me to leave and I said I would and I did and that's it. Live it. I live here now. I will survive on fish guts and fermented cigarette butts. Once in a while, a rich lady will buy me a frozen yogurt. The liquor store bitch will hopefully give me free lollipops and Funyuns ongoing.

Over there, sailors in white uniforms make an arch with their skinny swords. A bride and groom step through, the bride glowing like she's being born. The bridesmaids are in pink, perfectly coiffed hair devolved to ribbons flying wildly. Blinking hard, they struggle to look happy, a flashbulb is flashing, flowers are throttled.

The sunset is spectacular tonight, really, fast slashes of flame-orange as if gouged by sharp talons, against an elegant, serious violet. Some stars already disrobing, rolling their shoulders. I am a seasoned veteran of sunsets and not easily impressed but this one's a real crackerjack. Maybe I am losing my mind like Van Gogh, like how they say he painted the swirls around the stars in 'Starry Night' because that's how he actually saw things because he was crazy. The horizon swallows the final orange ridge of sun like a flopping gold fish. The bride and the groom make mouth contact, cheers erupt.

Not my mind, THE mind. Not my thoughts, THE thoughts. Not my ego, THE ego.

Not MY loss. THE loss. Not MY mother. THE mother. THE mother.

Cowboys

FUCK I'M AWAKE. I punch out from a mottled sleep, it's night, it's cold. Stomach is choppy, thick paint, my body is clenched. I feel like someone kicked me. Wanting to push through the shaky cobwebs and remember the root of this strange, thick heartbreak, I press my hand to my heart, press, press, press, like something will happen if you press this button, and indeed two shadow figures materialize before me. Cops. Yes I'll 'move along' you fucking dicks. No, wait, spectators. Tourists? Christian convincers? A man and a woman, both wearing cowboy hats? The woman has fringe hanging from her arms, her fists rest on her hips. The man has a big silver buckle on his belt. He points a gun at my face. Right at my face, and I'm thinking he'll end me and well, that was easy. That was fast. Only it's not a gun, it's his giant primate hand reaching for me, for my throat. A smoky desert rolls out behind them like a paper scroll. I close my eyes, hoping for a change of scenery when I re-open them, an easy restart, as in a lucid dream.

Alas the cowboys are still there. He grows in size like a dark cloud, a smudge. I roll away and he grabs me by the jacket. He is very strong. I can feel how strong he is, I am no match so I yield. He holds me by the arm.

Ouch, I say, casually, but feel a survival instinct pump something metallic into my blood. What could they want?

You sure it's her? the woman says.

It's her, the man says.

Is she high on something?

What are they going to do to me?

An overwhelming clamor, a great chopping, drops suddenly from above. The noise slices the air into squares. We all clap our palms to our ears. A helicopter descends, hovering low beside the pier, shining a bright light down into the water. Is such a bright light possible? It seems brighter than the sun. People collect on the pier, looking down over the edge. Their shapes are precise against the bright alien light. I've never seen a helicopter so close up before, I did not realize they were so big, a mechanical whale, it's almost silly.

They're looking for something, the cowboy woman yells.

I lie back down in the sand, back into the cast of my back, each vertebrae at home in its custom niche. Between the columns of the pier my eyes happen upon the coveted view, a limp dark animal being pulled into a Coast Guard raft, it looks like an octopus but I know it is a human body. From my throat comes a surprising laugh, a belched string of pearls, it comes and comes.

The Coast Guard raft (with the BODY) moves toward the shore unhurried, where a cluster of police cars and vans are waiting, people in long coats. A protocol. Coverage. The body came from somewhere and is going somewhere.

The helicopter disappears, the clamor fades.

I'm Jorge, the cowboy says.

I know, I say. I want to see him in the light.

This is Beverly, he says.

I'm his fiancée, she says. *Nice to meet you.*

Hello fiancée, I say.

We're going to look after you for the time being, he says.

He keeps his hand clamped to my upper arm. A hulking truck is our destination, new and sparkly with the words *Ramirez Plumbing* on the side. Now in the streetlight's glow I can see that he is real, existing in three dimensions, and he has the same cop moustache as on his driver's license, and almost an afro of thick black hair, and he is sort of terrifying in a movie star kind of way. I step on the truck's silver step and install myself into the small seat behind the front seats. I have sand in my mouth, my hair, my shoes, I did not shake out. The truck when ignited pants like an animal.

Death is not sad. Death is not death.
The spirit-body taking flight from the gross body.

The fiancée in the front seat has removed her cowboy hat revealing a huge mass of hair, and is playing with the radio. The man eats something crunchy from a plastic bag beside his seat. He digs and digs in the bag, pops into the mouth, a robot. The fiancée's hair tickles the side of my face but she does not notice. She cannot feel every strand of hair like a cat can with its whiskers.

I materialize Kaia in the seat opposite me, facing me. The coral headwrap, the white outfit, the powerful bird's eyes. She would be perfectly content here. She would not say, *Jesus Christ this is a small backseat*. She would not say, *What's up with the cowboy thing? Why do you both have such big hair?*

Miracles occur. Prayers across the map could open her eyes, send her on steady legs to the porch where she watches the moonglow illuminate the world, the little houses. Maybe the helicopter noise roused her. She takes a breath and feels hungry, she eats, she breathes, she lives, she waves her arms around to move her qi. She calls me back. I think I feel her calling me back.

Are you awake? It's almost 7, the man speaks to me in the morning, holding out a roll studded with raisins. I'm on the couch, it is so wonderful and comfortable. He is less like a cowboy now, he's wearing a white work shirt with a JORGE patch on it. I accept the food, put it in my mouth and try to clamp down, it's tough as a towel. I keep biting until I have a chunk in my mouth. The man squats next to me, his bobbing knees big as cantaloupes. He puts his hand on my forehead, a warm baseball mitt. His eyes are oily, wet, shifting.

I don't have a fever, I say.

Kaia passed, he says, spitting out words. *She died this morning, at home. It was peaceful. She was alone, like she wanted.*

The bread in my mouth is inedible now, as in a couch or guitar. He lifts me by the armpits, holds me tight to his big chest. He thinks I'm going to cry but what I do is vomit, a wild skinny snake leaping from my throat. I try to push away but he holds me, he thinks he should hold me, and the vomit soaks into both of our clothes and my hair. After a while I sink down into the floor, then farther, into a warm wet fish mouth.

There is puke on the wall, it is off-white.

There are the glowing numbers of the phone. And there is the dial tone.

But I cannot remember the number to the *Thoughtline*.

The numbers shiver and shift into foreign characters.

I don't speak a language

Feelings are never wrong

Eat something, THE COWBOY says. He feeds me one wet noodle, into my mouth like a mama bird feeding her baby. The night crawls slimily over the day.

She doesn't really look like you, does she? says Beverly, from the doorway. I am a specimen.

Communal Coffin

Kaia and I share a coffin. It's a coincidence, we just ended up together. Lucky us! So funny how our bodies are changing in here. It totally cracks

us

up.

Look, I just lost my last fingernail!
I just lost my lucky elbow!
Cackle cackle crackle.

Next we are the very top layer of the ocean, a foamy ghost one inch thick, holding hands. The ocean is a network of hands pushing and pulling, a single unbreakable net. We cannot talk but we are together.

People came from the ocean you know. They crawled up and out as teeny translucent frogs, too small to see, then they grew bigger and walked away from the shore and toward human civilization, shaking the water off, drying their webbed feet with small hotel towels. They kept walking, into restaurants, pharmacies, apartment complexes, and soon they populated and ruled the globe. By becoming the ocean again we are both the beginning and the end, the snake eating its tail, a baby girl born with all her eggs in her little pumpkin seed–size ovaries, the chicken, the egg, et cetera.

No, no, no. That is a myth. People came from corn, fully formed with hair in their armpits and libidos and favorite foods, but hushed, tiptoeing out of the dry stalks, moving their heads like owls, reverent, careful, quiet.

I am a dead seal on a pile of seaweed, mouth rotted open, the seaweed blossoms like flowers out of my eyes, my gums disintegrate to jelly and tiny flies feast on my remains, especially the corners of my mouth, until they are drunk.

When I am trying to relax into sleep I count passing spaceships, flat discs like tortillas with sparkling edges, they come toward me then move away, there is something in that flat round shape, I don't know why but it brings me close to home, close to her.

The Modern World

THINK SMARTBODY! THIS PREPARATION is formulated to maximize your body's natural detoxification system and clear cells of unwanted debris which over time can cause pervasive exhaustion, often misunderstood and misdiagnosed . . . Think SmartBody! In this modern world, processed food affords us great time-saving convenience but there is a cost . . . Think Smartbody! Only 10 percent of Americans get enough fiber in their diets naturally. There is no harm in supplementing, but there IS GREAT HARM in ignoring this common deficiency. Think SmartBody! Take control! Take control today!

A gray-brown moth is laboriously traversing the miserable living room. I've been following him on his journey. He's confused or injured, he crawls slowly over the vast ropey steppe, each fiber of rust-colored carpet a great challenge for him. His wings are clenched to his body, he is small, he looks like a dusty sunflower seed.

I am not allowed to make any 'noise disturbance' for two more hours, as per the house rules. Last night I extracted three books from their bedroom using the method of picking them out with eyes closed. Generally I like this method but this time I picked a terrible group: *Twelve Steps and Twelve Traditions*, (good but extensively explored already), *Get Fit At Home*, and *Introduction to the SmartBody Supplementary Nutritional System—Supplement your income through supplements THAT WORK!!!!*

In the cupboards are tubs of SmartBody vitamins, lots of them, but no food.

Which modern world? *This* modern world. In the fridge is a jar of grape leaves, cashew butter, margarine in a plastic tub, a bag of coffee, old milk, something in a styrofoam take-out box that I cannot identify, a few kinds of mustard, a few kinds of hot sauces, reds and greens. I lick some salt from the base of my thumb, the drumstick part. I prick a soft vitamin E tablet with a nail and squeeze some oil out of it. I touch the bead of oil to my tongue and it's not terrible but it's not food. When they get up we will all go to Salazar's and I can get a bellyfull of refried beans or maybe chilaquiles but they have to wake up first.

I could write or draw, but I just don't want to. I just don't want to. There are no good pens or paper here anywhere. There is no beach to go to or any place to just *be*. There is only *waiting*. I will try to sleep again, it's the kindest way to pass time, I'll lay myself back down, relax my skeleton and where will I go? On a floating mattress in the sky over the ocean, back over the pier. Put a sock over my eyes to block the light and feel the gentle movement, the gliding, induce the scene. Make small pink birds fly around. Make myself invisible.

Fuck it, I can't sleep. If there were ketchup I would stage a murder scene with me as the victim, just to scare them. But there is no ketchup, plus they would only be annoyed and make me clean everything up. Plus if there were ketchup I would eat it.

Advice

WELL I MEAN, DON'T you ever see your mind as being like a monkey in a cage? Like, literally? Like you're literally looking into the red eyes of this, like, insane mechanized overcaffeinated nonhuman primate? Approximately the size of two and a half housecats? Don't you want to make it lie down? Don't you want to *sedate it*? Show it who's boss? That's why people meditate. That's why there are seekers, why Kaia had followers. It's actually really simple—

I don't know what you're talking about, Beverly says. *My mind is not a monkey. My mind is like, I don't know . . . my mind is my mind. My mind is ME.*

No! That's exactly wrong! It's so great that that's NOT TRUE! Like . . .

She wants to read her wedding magazine and is so not interested in enlightenment. She wants me to leave her alone, she bought me a bag of peanut M&Ms so I would leave her alone, but there is nowhere to go. I have to make the present interesting. I study her—her fluffy reddish hair surrounds her tender skull like a fog, her lipstick is pink and shiny like a lollipop melting in the sun. Up close I can see the line around the jaw where her makeup ends and her real freckled skin begins, her bleached moustache, her lipstick bleeding into her face in tiny bloody whispers. Despite all her efforts she is still tired-looking.

Your eyebrows are a little bit uneven, I say.

Nice, now I'm getting beauty advice from a fucking hermaphrodite! She smacks down her

magazine. *What a world!*

Your mind is a pain in my ass!, she says after a while, and smiles at her cleverness.

THE COWBOYS LIVE IN a great beige condo complex with a communal pool. I guess I live there too. The pool is seldom used by the other condo people, and it's somewhere I've discovered that I can *be* so I go there a lot, wearing Beverly's hand-me-down one-piece swimsuit with tiny sunglasses printed all over it, floating like a turtle then getting out and drying in the too-hot sun, a towel over my head so the sun doesn't kill my face. Sometimes if I close my eyes and just float I can pretend that I am in the ocean.

At the bottom of the pool is a drain or something, round, and I like round things so much, and I like how this thing sucks my fingers toward it, like maybe it is calling me back home, maybe it's a supernatural invitation from Kaia, back to something more familiar. I have tried to step into the fold of this possibility but my desire for breath always sends me rocketing to the surface, desire for breath always wins. I made a guy on the second floor nervous, apparently he saw me in the pool from his balcony and thought I was drowning and starting yelling SAVE HER so now I am not allowed at the pool without a chaperone. Not drowning sir, just trying to. No, not really, but I'm an alien here, among the Hallmark cards, country music cassettes, snakeskin jackets, lambswool seat covers, AA tokens, shoe polish, women's magazines. None of it smells right. I envision walking soundlessly into the swirling night, why not? It's not remote, it's right there all glittering naked and beckoning me. But so far it has not happened, each morning I am still here, days strung together like pearls in a necklace, a boring boring necklace. Maybe I will adjust to it, my new home. Home. Maybe this is normal. Maybe I will become a cowboy too, a cowboy child of this condominium ghost town.

I deserve your compassion, I say. She looks up from her wedding magazine, she looks right at me but not comprehending, as if I have spoken in a foreign language.

Pink Matter

Like this, says Jorge, holding up a large pink rectangle. *If the blade gets dull, change it, and please don't cut yourself. Cut away from your body. Got that?*

Cut myself? I say.

I'm left alone in a large industrial warehouse, illuminated by the crack where the roll-up doors meet the ground and two clamp lights, two whimpering suns. Let's see if I can be an asset to the business, see if I know how to work. Yes let's see. A city lies before me, a city of great teetering cylinders of puffy pink material, cotton candy, almost as tall as me. There's a boombox which I crank, top forty! They built this city! I arrange the rolls, unroll some. I feel more alone now than I've been in a very long time, and I am filled with a strange tectonic-level happiness, it starts from the bottom of me and moves to the top. I feel inspired, silly, I dance to the bad music, I leap, and land, I do backbends using the pink stuff as landing pads. I had forgotten this flavor of corporeal joy, of goofiness, dancing with no observers, of having no concerns. Soon I'm breathlessly tired so I make a fort from the soft pink stuff, pulling a layer of it across the ground and another flat layer above and rest in the soft sandwich of darkness, disappearing where the pink meets the black, breathing like an animal, feeling the heat from my throat. Where the pink meets the black. I rest then rise again, moving a bit slower, more carefully. I create a pink martian moonscape, step over the hills and valleys open-armed, observing, sliding, turning the rocks over. I meet a mushroom that speaks. A family of giant sad flies. I excavate the caves and find the first poem, cut into mud at the bottom of a river.

My heart feels healed, or maybe just very light, a giant fluff of popcorn in my rib cage, a bridge made of paper. It does not feel heavy, anyway. I feel like Kaia is close to me today, watching me, delighted by me still. One time at the Del Mar Fair she and I entered a mother-daughter look-alike contest just for fun. We won the special look-*unalike* prize and got a bunch of free game tickets. I think that was the year we bought matching peacock-feather earrings at the fair, which I loved so much and was so sad when I lost one and then when the other one broke.

I'm sorry to bug you, I say, finding Jorge in the garage-office twitching his feet and concentrating on paperwork. *But I'm thirsty.*

Cutting 30 pieces in 4 hours is not a good *labor to time ratio.* This is a fact. Sure a person can play, in their *leisure* time, but that's *leisure* time, and leisure time is not all the time. Wouldn't that be nice? Wouldn't everyone like a life of pure leisure? There is a leisure class but unfortunately for us we are not a part of this class. Everyone here must contribute.

If I'm not going to *pull my weight*, I can wait for him in the back of the pickup. Enjoy a life of leisure in the back of a pickup, like a dog or maybe a paperweight. He wants me to feel bad, and I do, but just a little. My heart is unbreakable today. The black corrugated plastic of the truck bed is hot from the beating sun, too hot to touch. I protect my skin with my clothes and crawl in slowly, inch by inch, slow motion, take off my shirt and use it to cover my eyes.

Know the sensation. Do not fear the sensation. Do not cower from the sensation. Observe always. Let your heart be your compass.

A fixed shadow. A human heart carved from a bar of soap. A sundial in a great empty courtyard, an eerie echo, nobody is there. A well that goes down forever.

I wonder if anyone has ever been injured and achieved a perfectly round scar?

Household Poisons

TRAPPED IN MY BODY, I want to take good breaths but cannot. I am drowning in pain. My flesh is being chewed on, peeled away in strings. Particularly my hands, my fingers feel like flaming, pulsing matchheads. I've lost language, I can only thrash and shriek. I push the clothes off. I hear rustling, then the light clicks on and there is Beverly, in her pink pajamas.

Jesus, she says. *JORGE! Come here now please! She's . . .*

Jorge emerges, tying his bathrobe, looking down at me.

Let's get her dressed, he says, with a curl in his voice that means fear.

Come on now, says Beverly, trying to catch my foot into a pair of her white denim shorts. All my fingers look like thumbs, and are pink as flamingos.

At the hospital, the curtains that surround my bed are a watercolory peachy pink. I no longer feel any pain, I feel a soft cottony sensation, nourishing me in small waves like little hands. I feel my stretched and swollen skin, but it doesn't hurt me, it's only a fact.

Any new skin products, lotions, sunblock, bug repellent, anything like that? the doctor is asking them. My 'parents.' *Dish detergent, laundry detergent? Household poisons?* The doctor is a woman, with shiny black hair all the way down her back. She clasps the clipboard sweetly, with dark red fingernails. She takes my hand in her hand and her hand is cool and soft. *You're going to be fine*, she says. Is she wearing lipstick? Her mouth is full and rich like a plum, her skin almost like food in its urgent, dark, delicious appeal. I want to say something back, but my mouth is immobilized with dryness and shyness. For a moment I think she is going to bend down very slowly like an elevator and kiss me. *Water?* she asks, and motions for a nurse to get me some water. The nurse puts the straw in my mouth. Euphoria from my heart to my tips. The doctor reaches out to me and with one soft, perfect stroke, draws my hair away from my face.

This time I get the front seat of the truck, there's a first, and we go to Dairy Queen and I get a blizzard with Oreos. Jorge is quiet, head down, feeling guilty I imagine. His darkness emanates from him, his hollowness. I think he will say, I'm so sorry that happened to you. Any moment now he will say that. But no, it is not remorse that emanates from his body like a stink. It is only defeat.

Beverly does not think we 'needed to take her in,' Beverly is inserting a french fry into her horrible tender mouth without touching her lips, preserving her lipgloss.

It's important not to deviate, it's very important that I have no weirdness or tension about this, sometimes a lie is okay if it has the intention to do good. It is likely that they will ask 'leading questions,' it's really important to stick to the story. To concentrate. We do not have a lot of 'recourse' with these 'power brokers,' these 'rat bureaucrats.'

Jorge (but naturally I will say *Dad*) put me in a large quiet room in the same complex as his office (say 'office,' not 'garage') to do my schoolwork. In this same room was a bunch of insulation material, he told me explicitly not to touch it. I am being home-schooled because he prefers that to group education after having rigorously compared the two. (In fact, part of the reason he's self-employed is so that he can work his schedule around my education, he could make lots more money as an employee somewhere.) And then, typical of my character, I did not listen, I played around in the insulation material all day and then I lied about it because I was afraid of trouble and I am psychologically disturbed, having lost my mother not very long ago, and suddenly and weirdly. The thing about being told to cut the insulation, unsupervised, for an entire day, like I had told the doctor before? . . . well, this was a total fabrication, as they can see I have a very active imagination, you should hear some of the things I say, some of the things I come up with when I draw for God's sake! Elephants and aliens, sparkling ships and ghosts inside tortillas and talking mermaids, caves made of bones, I am clearly very smart and creative! Sometimes 'smart and creative' can lead right to trouble! Plus I was high on those painkillers when I said that stuff.

And if there is any doubt about what I am doing school-wise we will show them my books and my comics, and I am not going to mention that I have not made a comic or read anything or done anything with my brain since Kaia died. And maybe don't mention that I have not been provided any books or supplies and that the only thing I read is SmartBody propaganda. And if I could throw in some Eleanor Roosevelt quotes or reference some age-appropriate literature to show that I know things about the world, that would be great. And if I could appear happy and like I have a sense of humor and kind of 'lighten the tone of this whole thing', that would also be great.

I am taken shopping, bought a blue backpack with a leather bottom, a white button-down shirt, and a pair of purple-and-black checkered vans. Jorge puts one hand on my shoulder as we walk to the truck, this gesture of affection feels strange, like an ice cube being held against me.

In Sales

Danielle? This is Beverly, Beverly Weedman. Do you have a minute? Oh, boy, I bet, with those two little guys running around! Well, listen, I'll let you go, but I just wanted to check in about the supplements. The Daily 250 is what we have you on right? I know, isn't it great? Well, listen, I'm just calling because I figured you would like them, since everyone does, because let's face it they're a great product, and I wanted to let you know that if you did want to go ahead and order an ongoing supply, they're doing this promotion right now where you can . . . I know, I know, you're probably being pulled in a hundred directions right now aren't you? Oh, gosh, I can hear little Roger, is that Roger? Oh, hi Casey! Well if you want to order more I just want you to know that this is a great time because you can basically get a whole month for free, okay? So . . . do you want to go ahead and do that now? Well, you don't have to actually pay now, but you have to tell me for sure because I'm going to place your order . . . oh no? Oh really? Okay, well, I understand, but I highly recommend it, and um, if you want to do it let me know sometime before next Sunday if you want this special promotion deal, okay? Because it's going to run out. And I really do recommend it. Word of mouth, the best recommendation, right ? And there's a bunch of other things that we could talk about too—there are some protein powders and other products that are, you know, formulated for efficacy, and—okay, tell him I said hi. Take care now. Bye—okay, bye bye now. Bye.

She hangs up the phone.

Fucking fat bitch.

Cavities

If I had known you would have so many cavities, I never would have taken you to a dentist!, Jorge jokes as the truck bumps in and out of holes in the street. Serious-faced kids and dogs and cats scatter. I'm holding a white rag to my battered mouth, minding the endless pink drool. One-*third* the price, to get cavities filled in Tijuana!

My mouth feels stabbed, raw and tingly. I had required six fillings and we did them all at once. Kaia had not believed in dentistry, and had suspected that the mercury in fillings was poisonous.

You gotta admit that's pretty funny, says Jorge.

It'sh not funny, I say. *Ironic, perhapsh.*

I mean, what would she do? Take you to the dental shaman? Heeyah, hooyah, heeyah, hoooyah!

He cracks up at his impersonation. Sometimes he fake laughs through his nose and other times he really laughs. This time he's really laughing. He is in a great mood today.

We sit in traffic on our way to the U.S. border, surrounded by roving merchants who lumber slowly between the stopped cars in the cooking sun, wanting to wash our windows, sell us pillows, blankets, balloons in the form of Bart Simpson or Mickey Mouse. Bright roses bunched in plastic, strands of silver.

Buy your girl some roshes, I say, but he doesn't buy anything.

At last we approach the checkpoint, it's like a toll booth with a serious dude standing outside of it. I do my best to look terrified and beaten, hoping he'll think something weird is going on, pull us over, and something interesting might happen, maybe I can get reassigned a better life. I drool fresh blood, I let my head bob sideways like I'm barely conscious. Jorge licks his lips and sings,

Hello!

Authority makes him nervous. The man in uniform and aviator sunglasses looks at us for an instant then waves us through, one little flick of his hand toward his chest, the powerflick. He is fit and lean, a tight knot.

Fucking hate that shit, Jorge says. *Egomaniacs*.

You are free, act free.

That was a Kaia-ism that was very popular, very useful.

Someone got a tattoo of it, sent us a polaroid.

Equity

THEY WERE PLANNING TO wait until after the wedding to *purchase property* but you can't postpone life! This little gem of a place emerged, in the semi-country out by the rodeo arena, and they just snatched it up before they could overthink it. Why not? Everyone they know who has money made it in real estate, every month you're a renter you're building someone *else*'s equity. Someday they'll build a nicer house on the property, the real investment is the land itself. Five dusty acres, it extends to the top of a red rocky hill in back. The house itself, a shanty creature held up on bricks, is right on the road, as if waiting to be picked up by the garbage truck. I am not supposed to refer to it as a 'mobile home,' although it looks like what usually is referred to as a mobile home, it is to be called a 'modular home.'

I like the tire mountain, I say, because there is a pyramid of tires beside the house, at the top of the pyramid is a desiccated christmas tree with threads of glittering tinsel waving in the wind.

I'm glad you like it cuz that's your room, says Beverly.

It's no beauty but it's a good investment, says Jorge, and pinches Beverly's acid-washed-denim butt. *Kind of like someone else I know!*

We'll keep a few chickens, collect eggs every morning, put them gently into a basket, maybe have a goat or a hog. They will drink green tea from now on, no more coffee. They will really start using the five-hundred-dollar SmartBody juicer they bought. Beverly will take up jogging, seriously this time, she's already bought a subscription to *Runner's World*, and lose twenty pounds by the wedding.

I am not really going to live inside the pile of tires. There is a storage shed behind the house, halfway up the hill, and that's going to be my own little house. We're putting a big blue tarp over the roof so it won't leak, securing it with rocks around the edges, just for now. Jorge's up on the roof, I'm down here and my job is to find good rocks and throw them up at him. If I don't pay attention and throw well, the rock could fall back and hit me on the head, and this must be avoided. Another Child Protective Services incident would be bad for everyone.

The tarp is fine for now, but soon he'll put on a real sealed roof, and an indoor floor, and do a half bath. He'll install a motion-detector light. Someday he could possibly install an AC unit if I want. These things are all within reach, and he's happy to do it. He wants me to be comfortable here. He is in one of his happy ape moods. He will designate a certain amount of money every month for me, for books or whatever educational things I want. And let's stop calling it the storage shed, let's call it The Cottage or Nochita's Cottage or the Little House or La Casita, whatever I want. Let's even get me a set of free weights.

Plastic

Soon, sometime, I'll have a bed, but for now it's the cracked cement floor with a small stack of furniture blankets over a crackling sheet of plastic. Trying to get comfortable, I am a magnet for dark thoughts, they fall onto me like leaves. I don't fight them, I choose not to be alarmed. Not to be alone. To surrender. I can choose some things but I can't choose everything. I feel her body inside my body. My mouth is always full of her.

Hello, unsafe haunting ideas. Just what are you trying to teach me?

There are a lot of dead people around me, dead but alive. They are pretty terrifying. Lying in wait, undead, unkillable, in closets. I can feel them hiding and watching. Fingers twitching, tied to ironing boards, demi-deads forced upright. They've been killed a million times but never for good, and they look terrible! Hibernating, breathing like machines under the dirt. Lusty eyes, sweating lolling tongues. Paper tongues. I try to erase myself in order to be saved from their bloodlust, but like a fly trying to unstick from a sticky trap, my strength is nothing. Nothing. *You're not real*, I say. I try to erase them but I still feel them pulsing everywhere, wanting to strangle me like snakes. You can say yes and you can say no but sometimes you say no and it doesn't matter.

Out here, at night, the dark is extremely dark and the quiet is extremely quiet. When it gets dark, evil puffs up from under the rocks. Best to close my eyes hard and aim to go somewhere else. God is breathing through me. The zombies are freaking me out more and more, my constant sinister audience.

SHIT SHIT SHIT. THE zombies are winning. People sliced clean in half by swift bright blades. Sliced into ribbons. Surprised, mouths still open with shock, they are hung up on flagpoles by their hair. Dispossessed of shoes and handbags and business cards, chapstick. Jewelry cut off bluntly with crude tools and melted into bricks, sorted and stored in canvas-covered stacks. Sandals dangling from ankles. Blood drains, and bodies lose their freshness. Hands disintegrate, ancient bandages flap, guts dangle, flesh devolves into flakes. The hands reach stealthily for my throat, my ankles, my elbows, keeping pace, creeping. Poking me with sticks to keep me awake. Smearing me with fingertips. A sour bone hand around my throat.

Shit. To combat the assault of terrorizing images, I will call something to mind . . . a puppy bounding through a vibrant green field! This was something Kaia advised, picking up the mind and putting it elsewhere. Because you can! Because the mind is *plastic*. But the puppy, cresting a hill, is descended upon by a team of colossal black birds, one of them effortlessly lifting it. Uh-oh. Gotcha! A bird as big as a volcano, from the land of the volcano. Makes it look easy, makes the prey seem weightless. The birds are picking off prey left and right. A flapping snake, once proud but now pierced and hopeless in the talons, slowly expends and expires, stiffening then relaxing into gravity. The birds cluster and darken the sun, putting the known world in shadow like a sudden low rain cloud, rolling fast. The townspeople gasp, bolt their doors and clutch their children, hold their bonnets to their heads, scurry like disoriented ants. The birds' wings, if we zoom in closely, are made of enormous black feathers with an oily green sheen, each feather's spine is as fat and rigid as a ball point pen. These powerful wings pump the birds and their pathetic dribbling captives off to a place where pots boil over with muddy sludge, where puddles never dry, where sour, dripping jelly eyeballs are strung into necklaces and tongues are endlessly, hopelessly long.

Wake up with the taste of poison in my throat. Sleep is my escape. But I can't sleep all the time.

I did sleep all day today, or something like sleep. I was frozen like a human popsicle. I don't mean frozen as in cold, but clenched and still, like an object, a plank. So I can't sleep now, even though it is the time that people are supposed to sleep, the seed of night. I do my somatic practice then seek refuge outside the shed. I creep out where night is just beginning to dither into a moist, silver morning. I walk down to the road quietly, toe then heel. The birds are still there, lurking behind my head. A particular one of these asshole birds likes to taunt me, follow me, circle me. This time, on the desolate stretch of crumbly dirt road, she descends to my eye level, looks into me, flaps in front of my face, then ascends back up suddenly like a puppet yanked by her master, leaving her waxy smell, waxy sweet and slightly rancid, like Beverly's makeup drawer. I straighten up and try to walk confidently, because what else can I do? She dives back for me and stabs me right in the ear with her beak, sharp as a chef's knife. Drips of thin blood fall quickly down my neck, it was a significant puncture. I start to jog, holding my hand against my wound, looking around for shelter or a weapon but there's nothing, only low dry bushes, a torn-apart tire, a non-functional mailbox on a stick. The bird calls her friends, and a team of black beasts descends onto me in a single, twisting, chaotic body, now dropping down to my level, now clustering about my head and shoulders as I sway and swat uselessly, a boxer against an army. I bat at them with all my strength, hands open, big kicks, elbows too, but soon I am blinded, soon all I see is dirty black, stunned by the tart mildewy smell of their bodies at close range and the loudness of their shrieks deep in my ears. My resistance inflames them more. I give up. I'm so tired now, I feel like I'm floating. Maybe I've stopped breathing. Is this surrender? I feel no pain anymore, even though I know there's blood. Through a slice in the black obscurity surrounding me, I see the ground moving and something floating over it . . . my own dangling feet! I'm floating! They've lifted me by my jacket and are flying away with me, I've been captured. I want to laugh, the hysteria response again. I could fight myself out of my jacket and drop back down to earth but now we're so far up—it happened so quickly!—rooftops, pools like gems, the tops of palm trees . . . it's too late, even if I wanted to take the risk and fall, I cannot move now, I am as helpless as a scarecrow.

I don't panic. I breathe again. I get comfortable, tilt my head back to a more natural position and swallow the blood in my mouth, a mere teaspoon or two, salty and nutritious. This is surrender. *In our darkest hours we are the least alone. The others are with you.* When I close my eyes I can't really feel the motion. But when I look down I feel so dizzy! Yet it's a thrill to see down there, the freeways as a network of veins, we're passing over the sports stadium now, impressive in its perfect roundness, and so brightly lit, sending up vibrations of sunshine, even though it's night.

Me and Mr. Pinks

I PULL THE WHITE bucket full of slop from under the kitchen sink, take it up the hill toward the enclosure. It's heavy and hurts where it digs into my hands so I rest halfway, setting it down on the big rock. The animal sees me and is instantly electric with excitement, throwing himself against the fence and screaming. He screams so loud. He is a large animal and getting larger all the time. The fence shakes as I approach. I position my body in such a way that if he tries to attack me I might have the power to smash the bucket into his face, stunning him long enough to run back to the house and bolt the door before he devours me. I left the door to the house swinging open. I have a plan. But he could knock me down and eat the guts right out of me like a human trough before I have time to think, I bet. He's got the body mass of three of me at least, and he has that animal thing going for him. I overturn the bucket, plopping the slop into the modified industrial sink that serves as his feeding bin. Coffee grounds, eggshells, cantaloupe rinds, milk-soaked cereal, dry brown lettuce hearts. The effluvium of sour decay drifts up to my face and pokes holes in my brain. While I pour he seizes here and there, lunging and squealing, twisting and hopping. As soon as the slop is dribbling, the bucket nearly emptied, I hop back and away, but too fast, I spill putrid juice on my shoes and pants. It's the vomit of the earth, this juice. As I rinse the bucket, there's a safe distance between us, and I turn around to watch him eat. His jaws work fast, he's busy busy, his snout nudging corn cobs, turning them over, wanting the best stuff first. Root pig, root. His body trembles with focus, consuming as fast as he can.

The poor beast. Maybe I could grow to love him? He is a pleasant shade of pink, newborn-baby-ear-pink. Mud and shit are matted down around his feet and belly, clumpy around his wiry hairs. He's not so bad. He's just trying. He's just living his pig nature. He's got stringy hairy ears and a useless retarded tail and funny cleft feet and bad posture. Poor baby can't even dance. And then, we kill you and eat your face. I feel this alliance with him. How I am and am not like a pig.

Why do animals have tails anyway? I smack a pile of paper napkins on the kitchen table. Beverly moves them over a few inches. It's like a family dinner.

We're going to use the mirror tonight, she says, and places a small round mirror on the table, facing my seat.

I suck on a chunk of salty fish.

Look at yourself, she says. *Appetizing?*

I don't recognize a problem, I say. Slurp slurp. *You put too much lemon on the fish.*

You need to finish one bite before you start the next one, she says. *Let's start there. Do you get that? You don't open your mouth if there's still food in it. . . .*

We've been through it before. I put a squeezed lemon wedge over my teeth and growl. Beverly stops chewing and stares at me. Her eyes are flat and empty, her mouth shaky, and I wonder if she will start to cry. Or if she will slap me, or punch me. Or scratch me, one grand feline swipe bursting out of her soft chest, uncontrolled. She puts her fork down and rubs her eyes. She's wearing one of her fuzzy short-sleeved sweaters, the light pink one. They all have the same shape, a little globe around the shoulder. Jorge is still in the bedroom, doing something. Being alone with Beverly makes her hatred for me plain—we are here together, making a poisonous gas. It's simple: she would prefer me to disappear.

Honeeeey! She's not minding! she yells to Jorge.

Minding? Did you just seriously say I'm not <u>*minding*</u>*? Do people say that in this century?* I say.

Leave her alone, Nochita! Jorge yells back.

Beverly holds a fork in her fist. I'd like to dump her, scratching and sliding, out of a slippery bucket and into Mr. Pinks's food trough. He would turn her over with his snout and eat her globby butt first.

Daily Rites

When I wake up, I first notice if I am inhaling or exhaling, then observe my body's position and how it feels. Usually I'm on my left side, my legs bent and stacked. Sometimes my stomach is in liquidy pulses like gasoline mixing with sand in a bucket, swirling and swirling, dizzying fumes. Other times I have happiness in my bones, an electric celery stalk that grows through me and keeps growing and going. Also, it is freezing. Getting colder and colder every day. I try to let the discomfort run through me. A game, I try to remember what I'm wearing without looking. If I can't think of it I figure it out by feel. Jorge's old giant red flannel with the snaps. His old long underwear. When I get too cold I run around the room fifty times to warm myself, then settle back under the covers, feel my breath, the warmth blooming throughout my body, the pumping of the heart, filling the blanket with heat from my body, resting in the heat, I am a fat, warm flower.

Somatic practice begins directly under the skylight. I've become much more limber. Do I have a natural endowment or can anyone with enough time do this? When I first started I could not bend over and touch my toes but now I can touch my nose to my knees and put my hands nearly flat on the ground, and the ground is cold.

After the somatics, the sitting. I face the darkest wall for a while. One hour maybe. I don't mind the passing of hours and minutes, they are just little lizard tails whipping. The shadows and terrors descend and I hold the intention to let them *crest and subside* as much as they want to. Sometimes I sink into the earth or hover above the earth and that is all fine as long as breath is moving. I invert, place my legs in the air. When the sun warms my back it's an invitation to stop the ritual, and generally by then I have to pee.

I try to imagine them having sex, but my mind turns them instantly into pigs every time.

Sometimes they've left some coffee in the pot. I mix it with milk and have a cup. I throw away the filter and rinse out the pot. I fix a big bowl of cereal. I snap on the television, watch clumps of the news, soap operas. A group of people have taken to driving to the Mexican border and shining their headlights into the brush, to deter Mexicans from crossing over. There is a video of these people cheering as a group of Mexicans is loaded, ducking, into white Border Patrol vans, in the psychotic blare of the news crew's bright light.

Kaia in the sky with her golden telescope fixed on me, her hair floating like seaweed around her face. Her face as big as a billboard. Pride rising like a helium balloon in her birdcage chest, I can see it in her little smile. She knows I'm practicing. She sees me. She holds out her hand to me. She is not lost to me. We'll never touch, we're on opposite sides of the glass. Talking but not hearing. *Yes, my love!*, she mouths without sound, without even changing her face she conveys the comforting message to me. *I see you, you're doing great. Do that downward dog. Don't forget to do an inversion each day. Feel how vital you are. Feel the integrity.*

I do. I really do feel the integrity. My smallest components hopping like fleas, mixing with everything else in the great peppery buzz and the shake shake. I feel myself spilling and lifting beyond the borders of my skin, and I feel things entering me, too.

Sweet Steam

THE ASSHOLES ARE LONG gone when I descend the rocky hill to the house. They are like miserable paperweights on my spirit, pressing down the skin of the earth with their big stupid diesel truck, kicking up dirt in their wake and filling my lungs with it . . . yucky coughs. But they are gone now, for the day, and there is a sweet silence. I don't feel *them* in the house, it's a more general feeling of *people having been here* and it's nice, it's like warm laundry. Vestiges remain, dishes in the sink, bits of coffee and toast, shampoo-scented steam. I crawl into their alien bed and rest in their fluffy cloudlike covers and four great big pillows. Sometimes I put a pillow between my knees, sometimes under my knees. I just stay for a minute, just warming up there, I don't want to get too comfortable. I don't want my smell sinking in. I just want to be in this cloud for a second, then I'll go. I make sure I've left no hairs although they could not tell that it was my hair without close scrutiny.

On Jorge's dresser is a greeting card, the most macho greeting card in the world, the image is of a cowboy leaning against a fence looking down at his pointy boots, one arm resting up on the fence, a sunset behind him.

To my darling fiancé—Life is no perfect dream but I love you, and together we will find happiness. Your Cowgirl, Beverly.

This makes me surprisingly, terribly sad, a thin glass twig snaps in my heart. Two American commuters, trying for happiness, two vitamin eaters, wannabe cowboys, and will they ever find it? Jorge in his massive truck, heaving down the road, a manly slingshot's projectile that can't slow down or it will sink. Beverly in her glossy womanly bubble car, smiling at her diamond ring against the steering wheel. Polishing it with her toothbrush, kissing it, considering which shade to paint her nails.

The Happiest Day of a Woman's Life

A MAN ON A horse is presiding fiercely over a small green meadow. At first this statue is only slightly familiar, then in a wave I remember everything. *El Cid, it's you!* We'd had kind of a special thing for a while. Back in the day, when Kaia would bring me here, I'd climb up in his castle, I would dress up in his armor and clang around while he took afternoon naps. Sometimes I'd fall over, make a big sound and rouse him but he never would get angry with me, I think he liked my silliness, and liked that I was not afraid of him like everyone else. I would pour myself wine, thick as paint, into his gilded goblet and drink it up. It tasted like mashed sweet cherries.

He looks just the same again now, his feet in the stirrups just the same, eager and packed with power just the same. He is just about to thunder forth, stamp down limp, blood-drained bodies, feeding the soil with iron, flattened veins. There's no use getting upset about these tendencies. It's his very nature. You can't hate a cat for killing a bird. He's fierce, but he's got a pillow-soft heart for me. Does he look just the same, or is he a smidge smaller? A little cheaper-looking?

It's been too long since I've heard from you, he says coolly, and I guess his affection for me has expired, but then he invites me up. I can't though, I have to go to this dumb wedding right now. He looks at me, still as a statue.

He can't believe how I've grown. He can't believe, and neither can I, that I'm wearing a white dress with little red dots, snug so it accentuates what Beverly calls my *budding figure*, barfo. Barfola cola. He's looking at me. . . .

El Cid?! Appraising me sexually?! As in . . . as a *woman*?! I feel it, a red peppery poker into my spine. I'll turn right away from you!

Come back to me, he says. *Get up on my horse with me*.

Well I do. He helps me up, it's quite high up. Together we crush enemy bones to dust. Together we cross the whole earth, galloping over glaciers, flying over the oceans, icy breezes cut the sun. . . .

We have to do your face now! Stop talking to the statue!, Beverly yells from the RV, slicing my brain in half. She's always nicer to me in front of people.

We're in Eden, so our time is limited. The lush green park swells here and there into mild suggestions of hills, patted down and manicured into welcoming spots for sitting, eating, drinking, reading, watching a baby play. There's a big fig tree in the middle of the clearing, its branches sway gently and dapple the grass. Farther away, eucalyptus leaves shimmy, making a pleasant papery shuffling. In their shade, retired white couples amble in crisp white outfits, on their way to the bowling green. The tableau unfolds endlessly, a person could almost get hypnotized. Stop in place, and accidentally stay there forever. My dress makes my torso into a tube.

The "RV" is a humid, ratty little capsule of hell in the middle of this sweet heaven. From an upper bunk I watch as Beverly, assisted by her sister, prepares for the ceremony. This sister looks very much like Beverly except with short blonde hair instead of the brown fluff, and even more makeup, including possibly fake lashes. Beverly is giggling and bobbing like a puppet with a drunk puppetmaster, bubbling over with giddiness. The sister is laughing too, trying to get Beverly's leg into a tall purple suede boot using a very long shoehorn, it's not going well. Are they in fact intoxicated, or just so, so happy? There is a bottle of champagne and a bottle of sweet red syrup to mix with it. The happiest day of a woman's life. Once able to stand, Beverly examines her armpits, pinches her stockings, sheer with a stripe of violet sheen, twists around in front of the mirror to see her shoulders, revises her posture, shake shakes her tail, picks up the cluster of white roses, poses with them, smells them, puts them back on the table. She already brims with tears.

I can't stay still, I'll start crying, Beverly says. *Give me something to do.*

You seriously look like a model!, the sister says. *Okay, sit down. Hair!*

She teases Beverly's hair into a blown-back lionesque. With her makeup, she looks like a spraypainted embryo, heavy lips and eyes smacked onto a translucent, tender face. The sister plucks a hair from Beverly's chin. What strong wiry hairs can grown on the chin of such a soft woman! Every day new ones arrive like mattress springs poking out of a bed, sometimes I find them in the bathroom sink in the morning.

I don't think so, the sister says, staring deeply at Beverly's face. *I think we should choose either lips or eyes for drama, you can't do both or you'll look like a Tijuana whore.*

When the sister leaves in search of a diet coke, Beverly wipes her lipstick off with a napkin but some of the hot pinkness remains on her mouth.

Bitch, says Beverly. *Can't stand to see me happy*. She looks up at me. *There are some women like that*, she says. *Hey, do you like these stockings?*

Love them, I say.

I hope I'm not too casual, she says.

No way, I say. *You really do look like a model.*

This sends a visible flutter of joy through her body.

Woo! she says, shaking her shoulder. *Woo woo!*

Hey, let's put a little color on you, she says, and I give her my face. She applies frosty pink lipgloss to my mouth with a foamy wand, and silver eyeshadow, and puts coconutty-smelling stuff in my hair, it feels like a disguise.

Come on shake your body baby do the conga,
I know you can't control yourself any longer

The ceremony goes by fast and when it's over a big silver boombox emerges and pumps gritty radio beats, the small crowd dances on a fold-out dance floor set up on top of the grass. Jorge's father is there and looks very much like Jorge except with shock-white hair and a pipe sticking out of his mouth, more leathery skin, and an accent. He kissed me on the cheek when we met, and smelled of sweet woodsy smoke. I watch him pin a twenty-dollar bill to Beverly's shiny white shawl and take her hand, they dance together.

Feel the rhythm of the music getting stronger

I'm haunting the food table. One of Jorge's brothers invites me to touch his upper arm, something that feels like a stone is stuck under the skin. You can move it around.

It's not a bullet, it's just the scar tissue, he says.
But there was a bullet? I say.
Yeah.
In you? You got shot?
That's right.
They took out the bullet out?

That's right.

What's the story?

He shakes his head.

You can tell me, I say. I need to know.

Wrong place, wrong time, he says. He's got livewire eyes. I stick with him.

I don't want to meet my cousins. I don't want to dance either. I am shy and I don't belong here. I am not interested, except for the bullet man. My uncle. I want him to put his arm around me again. I will retreat to the RV and watch the party privately from the pill-shaped window in my upper bunk. If I think of something to do or say I'll come out. Beverly's sister enters the RV. Not realizing I'm there, she puts her head on the table and cries, I pretend to sleep. Wrong place wrong time. . . .

From the aluminum tray of one thousand enchiladas, I bring two fistfuls to El Cid, the red juice dripping down my arms and dress, he likes them and he likes the violence of my outfit, I drink red wine from his goblet until I fall asleep right at the table.

Maui

BEVERLY AND JORGE ARE in Maui on their 'honeymoon.' Another thing they could not exactly afford, but you have to *enjoy this life*, and Jorge had never been off this continent, unless you counted Vietnam.

I bike to the 7-11 down the road to find slop for poor, pathetic, wretched Mr. Pinks. I pick through the trash wearing a plastic bag on each hand. I find corn dog sticks with some food residue still on them, and a few cardboard boats of dry nachos. I keep biking, to the Rodeo parking lot, where there are overflowing trash barrels full of meat and bread and coleslaw and churros and pretzels, and in one bin I find a world of tamales, each one individually wrapped in plastic, I feel like the man who discovered gold. Back at home I unwrap and toss the tamales to Mr. Pinks like he's a seal and I'm his trainer tossing sardines. He is apoplectic with delight but never catches them because he is so fucking stupid. Poor dumb fucker. Corn lover. I dribble the remaining slop from the bucket into his putrid trough.

For you, my companion.

I'm less and less scared. If he kills me that seems okay.

Hello Doctor

IF I HAD TO go back to the doctor. It was so safe in there. The chocolate-haired, candy-fingernailed, sweet-skinned doctor. If she needed me to lie down. If I did, because I knew for certain that she was good. Because I trusted her. If I had to stay totally still and quiet. If she took my battered dried-up hand in her clean soft hands and said, what are these splinters from? If she came close enough that I could smell the perfume of her hair, aroma of a beautiful hotel. If she massaged my nodes so sweetly that I let out a happy closed-mouth sound. If she put her face into my face and pressed her ice-cream soft lips against my face, just next to my eye, and made me instantly drunk and then I plummet into somewhere new, but known . . .

Now it's someone else. A stranger is the patient on the table and I am floating above the scene and watching. The doctor puts her hands on the tops of the patient's chest, then the legs, pressing. The patient—a girl—something like a girl, but tall, and broad too, scared, but yielding. Too-perfect skin like latex paint. Closes her eyes.

Souvenir

THEY COME BACK SINGING and dancing like actors in a bouncing musical. They probably would have stepped over me like a rug but I wave and say, *Hi guys, how was it?*

It was perfect!, Beverly says, putting down her bags. She removes a purple orchid lei from around her neck and places it gently on the back of a chair.

Jorge pulls something out of a paper bag, hands it to me in a bunch. I open it, it's a pink t-shirt with MAUI! spraypainted across it, the bottom of the shirt is fringed and beaded. He's got warmth in his eyes, I feel it.

Thank you so much, I say. I'm considering embracing him, but it passes and then it's too late.

I picked it out, says Beverly.

The two of them in matching khaki shorts in front of velvet green mountains. Beverly on a boat wearing a large sunhat and a lifejacket. Beverly beaming up at the camera while bending to touch something in a river. Jorge floating in an inner tube in a hotel pool, sipping from a very long straw. Creatures under the water.

Free

*S*ERIOUSLY *I* DON'T KNOW *why you don't want to use the vita-tray,* Beverly says to Jorge. *Guess you want to do it the hard way.*

Jorge is concentrating hard, organizing vitamins into little groups on the kitchen table. He's making his 'optimal personal power formula daily.' There are many sizes and colors of pill. Each time a pill rolls off the table he catches it stealthily in his cupped hand. I am peeling masking tape up from the floor, because the new paint which I painted is now dry. I like the smell of the latex paint, and I like the possibilities of paint, how you can make a layer of new. I want Jorge to notice that I am doing something good.

I saw an accident yesterday, he says.

It feels like he's talking to someone else, but there is no one else.

Did I tell you already? he says.

Nope.

A car accident, really bad. It was right out there on Vista Drive. Two girls in a little convertible VW Rabbit, head on with a truck. It must have just happened, no cops or anything yet. The front of the car was just gone, just totally bashed in to nothing. The passenger girl was screaming about her teeth, about how they were floating in her mouth. She had blood all down her front like this. She was trying to get out of the car but she couldn't, she was jiggling and pushing the door with all her strength, screaming her head off.

I see the girl, the blood wet, solid, smooth and shining without interruption. An apron of blood. A vitamin pill drops from the table to the ground, Jorge picks it up quickly, blows on it.

But the other girl, the driver, wasn't struggling at all. She wasn't trying to get out. She was awake, conscious, looking around. She had this peaceful feeling. She had blood all over her front, too, all over her face.

But she was peaceful. She was mellow, I think because she knew she was dying.

Another vitamin drops to the floor with a soft tick.

Shit, he says.

But you don't actually know that she died, right?

She did. I read it in the paper, he says.

Do you know what they did with your mother's body? he says. *She wanted to be cremated. They sprinkled her into the ocean, off the pier. It's illegal but people do it.*

Maiden Voyage

After my nightly exercises I am centered and calm and all my weight is evenly distributed among my cells. I am in bed, covered like a child from neck to toesies with a furniture blanket, heavy with dampness, my hair spreads out like a dark flower. Without thought or design my skull fills with pictures of its favorite shape, the glittering tortilla, the spaceship, the round stadium, and it feels like something could happen, something magnetic and bright. In the space between asleep and awake I hear my name, whispered, by a voice that sounds like mine.

When the time is correct I begin digging with silent, steady fingers. In tiny increments and in no hurry I dig through the cement and the dirt and keep going and going. Just as I am beginning to wonder if anything is really there at all besides dirt and stones, I come upon a clear plastic sheet. I tear it open carefully, peel it away, I unearth her, stand her up, brush the dirt off crumb by crumb. She is dazzling, even in the darkness, she is brilliant. She barely needs the ground, she almost floats. She stands up straight like a knight. She takes a few tentative steps, like a baby deer just learning to walk, just seeing about it. Her mouth stays sealed. Her eyes are blank like a newborn's when everyone says, what color will they be?

Powers

I AM FLAT LIKE a cartoon. No need to open the door cuz I can slink through the bottom crack. I prefer to do it that way, more natural plus more fun. I dissolve and reassemble. I can make myself dark. I can make the whites of my eyes disappear. I can sound a rattle from inside me. I can make the plants stand back up after I've stepped on them so it looks like no one's foot has been there. I can make my palms radiate light.

When I arrive at the paved road I conjure a bicycle, switch on its headlight, mount, and begin to ride. It could dissolve beneath me into a rattling pile of sticks at any moment but it doesn't, it doesn't, it hasn't so far, and it's working so beautifully, I am skating on ice, flying without fuel, sailing.

Rolling out from beneath every bit of matter are dark horses and children, somersaulting, galloping to life. Asleep and awake, hair blowing all around, flapping up out of the shadows and whipping like flags then disappearing again, it's all moving fast.

A man and a woman are eating hot dogs at their dining room table, warm buttery light ringing out from their window. Oblivious to the darkness that flaps and twists all around their crooked house. Horses at rest, born into enclosures and set into a lifetime of innocent boredom, curl their lips in sympathetic greeting as I pass.

I continue to ride and ride and ride until the houses end, until the cars end and the weeds end and the road ends and everything ends, until my headlight is boring a hole through pure blackness. What will be next? A glint, the pearly gray shimmer on the curve of a neck, wings as broad as bedsheets extend. The enormous creature bobs around me, churning up a chilling wind, filling my ears, my eyes, filling my skull, choking me down. So big, he could pull my spine right up out of my body, carry it back to the nest for the little ones to sharpen their beaks on, but I am not afraid, I am down for whatever.

He dips in front of me, steadily flying in the beam of my headlight, just in front of me. He moves at the same speed I move so we are like two parts of the same animal, or two animals riding in tandem. Maybe he is using my headlight for something? To look for something? To rest his eyes? To look for bugs or other things to eat? Is he going to decide to prey upon me? Well I don't panic. Whatever. I don't fear the sight of my own entrails. Pink? Yellow? Orange? I will just read them like tea leaves. He continues to precede me, dipping and rising. He fills my vision. I am following him now. Together we move through temperature drops and humidity shifts, and my ears pop as the altitude changes, and I am aware that at any moment I could be flying off a cliff since I can't really see, and this gives me a bubbly little feeling.

Birds don't have butts.

Salt

I DON'T COVET WHAT those other kids have. I'll just turn over on my side. I have my very own apartment, my very own pig! My very own toilet, aka, the whole world!

Oh, but we have laughs. Don't we? Do we?

Oh, we have laughs.

Like when I said the beans were too salty and Beverly made me eat a handful of salt, then I puked into Pinks's bucket? And I wondered if he would eat it but I already knew he would, and he did, but without his usual eating gusto, with a kind of minor-note glumness, as if to say, *I'm sorry it's come to this. . . .*

Oh, you think up the most terrible examples! That was a terrible night. We were all so tired. That was the night that the tire blew out, and Beverly lost her wallet. And it wasn't a whole *handful of salt* for God's sake. It was maybe a teaspoon. You can't just take a picture of one terrible night and make a judgment on a family. Yes, that's right, I said family. I could use the word *daughter*. No you couldn't. Yes I could. No you couldn't. You've never been anyone's daughter.

I hate puking. One thing I hate is puking.

The thing to remember about suffering is how it always ends. You may not feel it but you can know it in your intellect, and you can hold on to that knowing like it's a little locket inside your heart.

Graces

WHERE WILL I GO tonight? What is up for tonight? After my exercises, my arms burning from the pushups, my heat ballooning inside my blanket, I let myself sink, I hear my own voice calling my name and then. . . .

Two girls zip toward me on twin bikes. They screech to a dusty halt at the tips of my raggedy white sneakers. They appear to be twins.

Your shoes are reeelly old, says one of them, staring down at my foot. She carries a big backpack, she squirms it around, rebounces it on her back. They both have long black capes that tickle the ground. I cannot discern their age.

Before they came I had been watching the sky, trying to evoke a squadron of floating tortillas with glittering edges that would slurp me up with invisible magnet-force . . . Maybe something like a stingray . . . and take me somewhere else, Maui, Paris, a tiny island somewhere with lavender fish . . . peel away layers of my brain and reset everything to a pure white wall. . . .

I am poked on the shoulder with a stick.

Ouch, I say. *Would you believe, these are the only shoes I have.*

Poor thing! says one, all sarcastic.

They both have hospital-short hair and pixie faces with drained robotic plainness. Big eyes like shining brown nuts. Maybe one is a smidge bigger than the other. They are staring at me.

We're not twins, says one. *If that's what you're thinking about.*

We're not even sisters, says the second.

And we're not girls, says the first.

Their bikes are identical and spindly like insects. My bike looks like a wooden boat shored-up next to their lithe creatures. They squint at it.

Look, I built this bike, okay? Don't judge me. I have to hide it under my bed. I don't even have a real bed, and I have a blue plastic tarpaulin for a ceiling, and my only friend is a pig. So don't give me a goddamn critique.

I don't know if they like me or if they are going to kill-and-eat me, but they want me to come to their house and I go, riding behind them, chugging to keep up. Their house, big, boring and suburban cadaver-beige from the outside, is, inside, a rich abandoned place with a cocked chandelier that hits you in the face when you walk in, disintegrating animal pelts laid over fungusy furniture, maybe ship parts, and a big hole in the floor of the second story. They've installed a slide to get to the first floor from the second. To go up, you climb up a rope with knots in it.

Our house has a bowling alley in the basement, says one. *Seriously.*

The other one fixes me a drink, a *proper* drink.

They prepare a cheese using boiled milk and lemon, squeezed in a cloth. It tastes like milk, only solid.

They bathe me in a tub with flecks of grain floating in the water.

It will help those bumps on your skin, one says. She scrubs my back roughly and I don't complain although she might be scraping my skin off.

They lay me, slack and naked, on a towel in a bowling lane. They pose me, extending my limbs in deliberate ways, while co-humming a ghosty tune. Then they bowl, a couple of lanes over. I feel the rumble of the rolling balls, the crash as they knock over the ancient splitting pins. My brain's smoke has seeped out and formed a cloud above me. Trust is irrelevant.

When I leave, dawn is inhaling her first breath, a chilly question mark covers the land, the tops of the cars, the pebbles, the warping dart boards in the rotting garages. Somewhere between the spirit world and the material world, the current whateverworld. The time-for-coffee world. The dawn is a smiling woman with smoky mysterious eyes and a wet pink tongue. I want to fold myself into every crack in every door, taste every flavor. Strangers are everywhere! This creates a flapping joy in my chest, which I convert into energy, pedaling faster and faster on my wooden boat-bike. So when I hit a bump and fall off my bike and do a full tumble before my face comes to rest in a soft patch of acrid horse apples, I enjoy it more than average. I just stay there.

You have to make your own world, one untwin had said while voiding the sponge over my head in the bath. *And you can't trust adults.*

I know, I said.

I just feel totally trapped, I said. *I know it's stupid, I know that there is no such thing as 'trapped.' I know my spirit could be free. . . .*

Live with us, the other one said. *Be with us, see? Don't be such a dopey mope.*

Yeah, you could be our maid, said the other.

They do need a maid. The place smelled like dirty dishes. I get back "home" in time to see Jorge climbing carefully into his truck with his commuter mug and lunch cooler in hand, official in his white white uniform, a member of the public army. He carries his sadness in his spine. And my poor hysterical beast, you know, the pink one with the curly tail and the mucus mask, is hysterically hungry, being very vocal about it, and I promise him a fresh bucket of putrefactissimo very soon.

Jorge and Beverly come home with bright white teeth.
We treated ourselves, she says.

Evil Eye

Beverly is still upset because some days ago when we were at the drugstore I asked her if she needed more moustache bleach, and she thought I said it intentionally loudly and that someone had heard. And that someone specifically was a smirking handsome young cowboy. *And then you wonder why we don't take you out more.*

She is cooking her trademark chili and I am standing behind her and then out of nowhere her elbow jerks and she flicks something at my face. It's red pepper powder, I can taste it, it is sweet for a moment before it begins to throb and then lacerate in the slits of my closed eyes, I dip out of sight, outside, turn on the hose, put my face in the heavy cool stream, closing my eyes. It feels like glass. The heat pulses in my eyes and then in my nose and a little bit in my gums and it pulses hotter and hotter and I know it will pass, I just hold on, the pain becomes unbearable and I want to scream but I don't. I scream inside and I peel Beverly's face off with her evil eye still buzzing, I throw the quivering mask to Mr. Pinks, his favorite.

Hand-Gun

YES, I CAN HOLD it. Go ahead and hold it. I make a platter with my two upturned hands, and Jorge places it there slowly, ritualistically, barrel pointed away from me. It's heavier than I expected. I keep it there, like I'm making an offering. This is a tender moment we are sharing. My brain jots it down.

It's a .38, Jorge says.

Yeah?

That means the caliber is point three eight inches in diameter.

Yeah?

Yeah. If you were interested in owning a gun, I would start you with a .22. Something small. Not so scary.

This one's scary. It's black and sleek like a short-haired dog from hell. I turn it over. I touch the trigger very softly. There is a kind of bright dissonance just then, a palpable, electric wrongness to this particular object in my hands, like those magnets that repel. Guess I'm a hippy kid after all.

Don't point it at me, he says, and pulls the barrel so it's facing away from both us.

It's not loaded, though, I say. *Right?*

Don't point it at me, did you hear me? I don't care if it's not loaded. That's how accidents happen. You think it's not loaded.

He's so into this. It would make him happy if I wanted a gun. We could connect over it. But I know better. I know it would lead nowhere fast.

After my pushups, I burrow into the blankets. I endeavor to occupy total silence and blackness. The gun smokes up my brain, haunts me, smiling, sinister. If I were crazy I would say the sleek beast was calling, beckoning me with one silent curling, trigger-shaped finger . . . *come closer, come closer. Put your tongue on me. Taste me.* I wish I could go back and untouch it, erase how I touched it, because something dark stayed on my hands, some shadow. *If you were interested in owning a gun.*

Something small, not so scary.
The way he laid it in my hands, holy water.

Woods

I HACK AT THE wood with the axe until I get something that looks like firewood. I bring the wood inside the house and start the fire in the potbellied stove with one match.

If I touched that stove when it's hot my hand would melt like a candle. I'm not good at cutting the wood. I hate cutting the wood but the alternative is that I hold the wood while Jorge splits the wood with an axe, and I have to trust that he will not cut off my fingers and I do not have that trust. So I cut the wood.

It's cold in this pathetic 'cottage.' I don't have a stove to keep warm like they do in the house. I cover my head with t-shirts like an exotic prince and jump around or if I'm in bed and don't want to get out I do the bed-cycle, which if you don't know is a kind of bicycling while in bed. Soon Jorge will put in a heating unit. But he is not feeling too well right now so I don't bother him about it.

Elevator

They're raising her up on two slender wooden poles.

Her body is broken but her spirit is still intact, bucking, kicking, fighting. Eyes closed, like on the doctor's table. Her shirt has fallen loose and one of her strong shoulders is bare, lending to the scene a twinkle of uncomfortable eros.

The crowd is trained on her writhing form, her ghastly performance. The best performance. They want to see her licked away, melted like butter then dried and bubbled into black ash. Then they will go home and roast a nice shiny chicken.

The stakes are steadied, straight up now. The dry grass is lit beneath her body. The slavering crowd is transfixed as the flames crawl up the stakes toward her feet.

But then the tight concentration is broken, there is an unfamiliar movement, a kind of visual buzzing. Something like two flickering moths appear in the distance, first twittering on the horizon then becoming larger, becoming a speedy tangle of meaty leg and grimace and coarse hair. Two dark beasts sprint toward the mob, terrifying in their determination and the thickness of their thighs. This is a military operation, it's force. The crowd is freaked out by this, they're gathering their things, thinning out. The dogs, they are some kind of very serious dog, tumble to a stop right at the fire, scattering dirt and rocks and smoke.

The elevated person is bent like an arc, is mewing like an animal, stiffening like she's trying to coil up, then slackening back. Already the back of her dress has turned brown from the heat and her skin has begun to blister. Her belly is pulsing with little breaths.

The dogs' eyes are clouded over, white-blue, sightless. They find the stakes by smell and rip them furiously out of the ground, sending up a cloud of dust. The woman plummets to the earth, her hair and dress rippling. Just as she is about to collide with the ground, her impact is softened by the dogs' backs as they move in precisely to break her fall, catching her. She is draped over their backs as they walk slowly away, stepping in tandem, an ancient ambulance. Her tattered, caramelized dress drags in the dirt, she breathes through her teeth. They carry her into the wet dark forest. They lay her down in soft dirt, cover her eyes with her hair, soothe her burns with damp, healing leaves.

Amigos

Sometimes when he is furrowbrowed over his AA book or over the vita-tray making his daily formulas or cleaning his gun, when the sadness rolls off him in tired puffs, I have an impulse to reach out to him, put my arm around him. In his shoulders he carries a vestige of the high school football star he once was, and that's where I put my hand. I imagine him putting his hand on my hand, saying *yes*, and us being friends. Maybe we put our heads together. I feel the possibility of friendship, of an opening, of moving through the discomfort and into something better. We could have been friends under different circumstances. If we were two strangers, meeting randomly at a gas station or a Denny's late at night. I would make a little joke, like maybe the waitress would serve him a hamburger with fries and a side of ranch dressing and a shake and I'd look over and say, 'Just a little light snack tonight?' and he would laugh. We'd be unlikely pals, happy hobos. We'd go for walks, tell each other everything. Things would get serious and he'd tell me about Vietnam, how he went there thinking it would be a certain way and it was actually nothing like that and people were worse than he'd ever imagined possible and he got his heart broken so deep he never got up from it and he's just been limping along ever since. I'd tell him about my mother, a new-age guru with these tooty frooty followers who asked us for chunks of her shit and hair to meditate with. I'd tell him about the time I accidentally took LSD when I was six, having eaten some sugar cubes I'd found in the backseat of our Bug while waiting for Kaia, and I'd thought I was inside that book 'Frog and Toad Together,' I was a frog on a lily pad, I mean not just ON a lily pad but like, inside it. He'd tell me about growing up sharing a bed with two younger brothers. We'd be serious and silly both. We'd go to Salazar's for nachos then proudly make resounding farts. He'd say, no way you're thirteen, you've got to be twenty. I have an old soul, I'd tell him. Happy hobos, writing notes with crayons, shoplifting. I'd make fun of his moustache. I'd make fun of his 'Trucker Hits' cassette tape although I really like that one song "Still Willin'."

That kind of friendship seems possible but always slips just out of our hands, maybe we are not brave or kind enough, maybe we are not ready, maybe we just don't like each other.

Potential Trajectory

THE BED IS COVERED in blood and bits, dark dashes spattered over all four walls like frantic punctuation. The blood soaks through the bed entirely, saturating it like a sponge. Jorge's body drained and small, now made of greenish powdery clay, his empty eyes rolled upward like an ecstatic religious statue. He's still clutching a pillow with his desiccated mummy fingers. I pry his stiff fingers from it.

I run from the shed to the house, toward him. I leap from rock to rock, I swing open the weightless bedroom door. He is there, he is alive, sitting on the edge of the bed. His eyes roll around to me, meeting my eyes but communicating nothing, bovine. A dial tone. The sheets twist around his legs like an exhausted diaper. Otherwise he is naked. His belly is droopy, slack.

Cover yourself, Jorge. I can see your privates.

He doesn't move.

Are you sick?

Nothing.

Of course, there it is—in his flaccid hand is the new gun, clean and shining. It rests on the bed, pointing at my thighs. I step sideways so I'm out of its path.

Don't point it at me, I say. *Right?*

Nothing.

I'm going to take that away.

I reach down, clasp the barrel, repoint it. His finger is on the trigger. I tug, tug toward the wall. But he doesn't let me have it. Even his indecisive, limp grip is strong enough to defeat my effort. His eyes are filling with greasy tears.

I relapsed, he says, in a different voice than his usual. *At the conference.*

A tropical-themed motel room. Jorge inverts a bottle of wine, glugging while a ceiling fan rotates slowly above. A lady is on the bed rubbing her legs together like an insect. Reno.

Give me the gun, I say, and tug harder.

An odd sound, dried-up, a gaspy cough that could be fake. A paper crumpling, something like laughter. He's weeping! I put my hand on his shoulder and move it back and forth like rubbing spices into a piece of meat. He releases the gun, putting his hands to his face, and I pull the gun away. I point it at the floor.

I don't want to do it anymore, he says. He pats around for the gun. The gun.

I took pain pills, he says. *I took this woman's pain pills at the convention. I washed them down with vodka.*

I rub, rub the shoulder. I want to say something so good.

In the big picture . . . that doesn't seem like a huge deal, I offer.

I'm tired. I'm old.

You're not old, I say.

I'm sick of it.

Beverly opens the door, wearing her new exercise outfit.

I got the new—

She steps back. Her eyes scan the room, taking in the scene—Jorge naked, slouched on the bed, pounding his eyes lightly with his fists, weeping. The gun in my hand, pointing at the floor. My hand on his back.

Is that loaded? she asks.
I don't know, I say. Probably.
It's loaded, says Jorge.
He's sick, I say.
She finishes scanning the room.
She says, *Should we go to the VA?*

ALMOST CATATONIC IN THE hospital bed, he gives his hand to a nurse like an injured dog offering his limp, stung paw. The nurse wraps a paper bracelet around his wrist, clasps it closed, pats his hand then disappears.

Be good, I say. *Get some rest. Don't be an asshole.* His eyes roll up to the ceiling and down to the ground. He smiles the tiniest bit. I wanted to make him laugh.

You're going to get better, Beverly says from the doorway, almost a threat.

I wonder if the nurse who put the bracelet on will feed him from a can of 'fruit cocktail.' This picture—Jorge's mouth barely open, a syrup-soaked grape or a cube of pear being spooned in—fills me with such acute sadness and dread that my heart and stomach turn heavy, turn over to stone, and my eyes fill instantly with tears. In that moment I feel a shard of his terrible sadness, a shining blade expanding inside my ribs.

At home, Beverly is crying like a gurgling drain at the kitchen table. The gun is still on the bed where I left it, in the messy swirl of sheets. I put it in its shoebox, place it on the top shelf in their closet.

We're getting rid of those, Beverly says. *All of them.*

After I make up the bed, I collect them. I find all of them. A woman should know how to protect herself. Beverly's gun too, which has a pearly handle and is kept in her panty drawer. Even the lame-looking blue plastic BB gun is outta here. I've touched the BB gun once before, when Jorge was trying to show me how to shoot at cans when we first moved here and I shot once, nearly pegging the neighbor's Siamese cat, and Jorge laughed so hard, his real laugh. I should remember that more often.

Beverly frames herself in the window.

I'm so sick of this, she says, an actress practicing a line. *It's hard for me, too.*

She disbands the stirrups from her feet and crawls into the bed.

I must be a decent person because if there was something I could do to help her, I would.

Blood

A LIFE OF SUFFERING and desperation and then a loveless, graceless death. Mopped up with foamy chemicals by workers in white suits. The unsalable parts of you discarded with no affection.

I'll treat you tenderly, I say, tossing Pinks a cabbage heart. *You can count on me.*

But I cannot think of a viable rescue. I could open his gate and just let him run off like he wants to do. But of course then he would die on the road, run over by a three-ton truck or a van full of kids with special needs, or be trampled by a spooked horse. He would die frantic with dark blood dripping. Blood dried on his snout. Brown blood. Oh, that's no way for my big old baby to die. Maybe a bleach-reeking slaughterhouse is not such a terrible lift-off. *Is it, now, my big baby? Such a terrible lift off?* He bows and munches. Bow and munch, nudge and crunch. Pig nature. They know what they are doing there, it will be fast.

Mr. Pinks, A Pig. Rest in Peace. He died as he lived—hysterical.

JORGE COMES BACK FROM the hospital thinner and happier and with an addiction to cigarettes. He's going to stay thinner, stay on his medications, he sees no need to weigh over two hundred pounds ever again. He's going to more AA meetings, and he's going to talk about his feelings more. *Nothing noble about suffering in silence*. For his homecoming, Beverly tied a balloon to his chair.

All we can do is try.

Beverly makes dinner. Pork chops!

Us

THIS IS ESCAPE?

My feet hurt, I have blisters the size of golf balls already.

We are walking very quietly. The land around us creeps darker and darker, the lights decay. Soft amber handfuls of comets falling, lanterns floating slowly down a river. I don't have energy to think about it. I am putting everything I have into continuing to walk despite the crushing, overwhelming exhaustion. Breathing is an effort. I sense him at my left, the one I am supposed to be following, half a step ahead. Almost certainly he wants me to pick up the clip a little. Almost certainly I'm the one slowing us down. We don't work it out, we conserve. He is visibly tired too, and soon, like me, he is walking on feet and hands to distribute the pain. The pads of my hands get quickly bloody and the dry pebbly dirt is entering my bloodstream, maybe that's why I'm dizzy and funny, maybe that's why the occasional headlights are turning to orange smears in a swirly soup. I feel the pricks of insects on my calves and ankles but have no energy to swat them away. The air is thick like muddy water. I don't know if the night is warm or cool, I don't know if there's any wind, I only know that I step, and after I step I step, I step, I step, et cetera, and the end is not particularly near, so there's no use wanting it. Soon I cannot even lift my head, and soon after that my mouth begins to loll open, I don't have the force to snap it back up. When my tongue touches the ground it wakes me up rudely with the sudden texture. I don't want to eat any of the ants, I can see that some of them are carrying glowing white eggs on their backs and I bet they are nutritious but I don't want them.

When a stray stripe of light passes over and illuminates things for a brief moment, I see that my hands have changed. My wrists are thinner, my fingers smaller and more curved, and my veins stand out, straining little cylinders. My breathing is getting hotter and louder in my head, the acoustics of my skull are shifting. My fingernails have changed too, they are narrower, thicker and more tubular, and my skin has a sheen, has grown short coarse fur. A nice graphite sheen. These changes are happening as I watch. I don't feel any anxiety about any of this, I am moving toward some kind of freedom. I touch my head and know that my face has changed too, it's growing a lupine point, I had suspected so.

Others slink out of the dark brush to walk with us. Soon I've lost him, my guide, I don't know which one he is, we all look the same, a soundless army, walking at the same pace. There are more bugs now, wanting to drink from my new wet eyes, trying to fly up my nose. Some are big, junebugs maybe, or beetles, they multiply and buzz around my head like a maddened halo. Some of them are as large as small birds. I bat at them but my hands, now that they are paws and not hands, have no lateral movement, and I'm sure I look very foolish.

It's the seed of darkness. In the egg-still center of night even the birds are still, sleeping and dreaming bird-dreams about shiny bloody berries and good twigs. Everyone sleeps except us. We pass through the neighborhood of dark homes, a shuffling pageant of thin ropey spines, lean muscly rumps and bedraggled steps, a slow, tired cloud. How many are we? Well we have no visible beginning or end. I feel I am part of a river, our will is shared.

Now we pad through the parking lot of the rodeo, sinister and epically empty, then on across the silenced highway, to the industrial zone full of boxy warehouses and roll-up doors, to the immense *panadería* which covers a whole block and is very austere like the surrounding buildings but does have a few windows with red and pink trim around them. Some in our pack stop there, noses slowly circling, hypnotized by the perfect smell of sugar bubbling in lard, of sweet, dyed batter rising in molds. There are two women workers visible inside, wearing white aprons and hats, sliding great trays onto multi-tiered carts, wheeling things here and there. They do not appear to see us, it must be that they don't see us, or they would be screaming and crossing themselves and flour would be flying everywhere. The smell is too much, its thick vanilla perfume enters me, slugs me. My thighs quake and threaten to buckle.

The wolves, we wolves, have formed a triangle now in front of the closed doors, like a military formation but not threatening, just floating there, passively persistent.

Does she see us? The younger one, with the big gold earrings? She seems a little different now, as if she's noticed us. She's dragging an immense black garbage bag from the back to the front, she unlocks the doors and pushes them open. She uses all her strength to lift the bag and heave its contents outward, raining sweets upon our mangy mass, hurling buns and soft cookies and cream-filled cones into the air. She shakes the bag until it's empty, pulls the door shut and locks it again quickly, scurries back to work. Bright pink cookie disks are ground to powder between strong jaws, buns are bounced eagerly down throats and choked down half-chewed, crumbs are exploded in arcs onto the sidewalk then licked up by fervent tongues. I enjoy an almond crescent that had landed between the spokes of an abandoned motorcycle. I lick crumbs from between my tight toes. The moment arrives when there is nothing left, really nothing, not even one crumb floating in a black gutter to be consumed, and so we move again. We are an ugly bunch, skinny balding tails, visible bones, damaged eyes, dirty drumstick legs. But at least now we are a pinch more animated, holding our heads a little higher.

At dawn I drink from the same shallow puddle as a horrible pigeon with one leg like a french fry and the other one fissured and bleeding. I swat her and start to eat her, but she tastes dry and dirty so I spit her out. Hey, I'm new at this! I nudge her body into a bush to rot, thieves' honor, then jog to rejoin the others. I break again from the group, slink down the rough canyon wall, the dry brush scratching my new fur. I have lost my fear of falling and am enjoying experimenting with this new lawlessness—I toss myself like a ball down the steep slope and I simply do not fall. My limbs are quick and my built-in shoes do not tumble or slip. I have no language but I have a dignity. Birds flap away from me, alarmed. I consider killing for sport. I'm hungry but I don't want these gabby dirty city birds with their fungusy feathers and beaks. I don't want to drink coarse salty bird blood. I want something fancier.

Red Army

Holy fucking fuck!

This is not an apocryphal scenario!

There is actual blood! Like if you were hurt! You fucking drip blood!

A different sort of blood, but definitely blood. Even gorier than the regular kind, sometimes meaty and black bits and sometimes fresh and thin like a watery nosebleed.

All those women you see walking around? They're all bleeding into things, blossoming their butterfly blood stamps, tamping products into their panties, tending, checking, washing, wrapping, plugging, discarding, caretaking. Unrolling, changing bandages. A secret army. I can't believe this. It can't be real. This is too weird. Something must be wrong. One in four. Bleeding. Dripping. Their guts slithering out. There must be some mistake.

You pull a tissue out of the box and another one is already ready. That's how money comes out of my mouth, ears, eyes, that's why they keep me around. I'll go forth on my rattling bike, crawl under someone's house to rest and hide, entomb myself until they forget me. Then I'll resurrect, fling into the world, find my people hiding in gas station bathrooms brushing their teeth with their fingers. Drinking pancake batter around the campfire. I'll find them, I'll make a life.

If I left, Beverly would drag herself into that pawn shop so low, so low. A howling, bedraggled animal hocking her engagement set. The diamond goes *click* when she puts it on the counter, poor doll. She can't even meet his eyes.

Oh, they're not so terrible. They're just people. Just small-time, small-town vitamin pushers. Anyway, I can leave whenever I want, and I will leave soon, I'm waiting for the moment when I am called.

I really have to shit but I don't want to enter the house unless those people are gone, and they are still there, unless I missed their leaving when I was inverted or dancing?

No, they're here. Because there, in front of the house, is Jorge's glittering monster truck, unawakened, and next to it the womanly convertible, glittering red. Cute couple!

I can't wait anymore, so I enter the house. It's cold, silent, and still. No voices, no swish of clothing or jangle of keys, no coffee, no shower steam. Could they both still be sleeping? Could it be earlier than it feels?

I cannot think until I relieve myself, producing an impressive outcome with a clean, decisive finish.

I knock on the bedroom door. It's closed but not completely. I press open the door.

Hello?

The walls are covered in stripes of shadows from the blinds. Hanging out of a shiny black dresser drawer like a vulgar tongue is Beverly's purple sweater. A white sock hangs out of the lip of the hamper, next to the hamper are Jorge's brown work boots with the laces stuffed inside like he likes. And hanging from the closet door is today's white shirt, pressed, with his name. Jorge.

Oh dear.

In death they are smaller, maybe 75 percent of themselves. Effigies, models. Wax people with pink cheeks. Cultists, maybe, the way they stare straight up with their hands stiffly at their sides. Having gone with purpose, destiny, ritual. Hairless cats, unwrapped mummies. Presented to me for dissection or study. They are on the bed, staring at the water stains on the ceiling.

Hey come on, what are you guys DOING?

Her foot, a luminous white marble. Her toes marbled beans. I touch one. It's cool.

I look around for clues, enforcing slowness. My hands hold out in front of me like cameras. There is the green shaggy ruglet scrappily embracing the bottom of the toilet, the matching toilet lid cover. There is the medicine cabinet, divided in half, his and hers. On his side is shaving gel, an electric razor, tiny scissors, toothpaste, floss, tiger balm, generic petroleum jelly, Tylenol, an antique water-stained box of Band-Aids. Her side has tweezers buttoned in a velvety black pocket, Smartbody vitamin E oil in a tall bottle, cocoa butter, talcum powder, a dingy makeup bag, a little pile of jewelry. On top of their dresser is the little basket with keys and coins and AA tokens and a broken watch. There is the smoke detector with its blinking red eye, the kitchen table with big jars of vitamins, the woven bowl holding two onions and a lemon.

Trash under the sink. Chicken bones, plastic wrap, bean cans, wadded paper towels. Last night they wiped the grease from their lips onto those. The dish rack is full. The dishes are dry. The wooden walls squat and breathe, pressing into my chest. There is no pain. This is a very small house. Nothing is uncommon, unusual, apart from two very tidy corpses. A hollowness is all. And the cold, colder than usual.

I use thumb and forefinger together to pull down both papery lids at once, something I've seen somewhere, a Western movie maybe. Beverly has perfect shiny red fingernails, all the same length and egg-shaped. Is it true they keep growing after death? And what an engagement set. The diamond sets fire to itself, inside itself, it throws light around. Maybe I understand about diamonds now.

They hold onto the sheet, rising together. They are missing. They are dead, but they cannot be dead. It was too fast, too quiet, like a tablecloth ripped from under a set table, a magic trick. Waxy make-up, too thick even for the stage.

Apocalypso

Rapturous lift-off in a sleigh, a peacock's feathers sprung open, vulgar flowers flash hot, the end at last. Houses are kicked over and throats are slashed clean and purple tongues are lopped off and neighbors talk and say:

I always knew that one was an adulterer, that one a liar.

Some people are lifted by the necks, others sucked down into golden veins below the dirt. The girl is there again, her hair rising up around her head then twisting like a frozen yogurt swirl, then she is pulled upwards and away, her face blank the whole time and her arms slack. Some disappear, erased cell by cell to reappear elsewhere, stiff and surprised. Some are grabbed around the waist by a giant fist, like King Kong, and lifted. Some are just squeezed dead. Some wake up with canvas bags of golden coins in their grip. Crack their knuckles and shake their heads. Some are treated lovingly and carefully, squeezed, but not too hard.

Patient Belongings

Jorge's giant handshake, the occasional clap on the back. When I could feel him.

At the car wash, a long time ago when we were washing the truck, he put the car vacuum to my face. He put me in a headlock, sucking my cheeks into the vacuum mouth. I had screamed and yes, cried. He was laughing harder than I'd ever seen him laugh, his eyes watered and he wiped them with his snot-pocked red hanky. He was howling like a hysteric even as we drove away from the car wash, and I was laughing and crying too. He gave me his hanky and even though it had his wet snot in it I took it and blew my nose and it felt brotherly.

The time he showed me the photograph of him lying down with a tiny baby on his chest, and the baby was me, and he looked delighted, purely delighted, at my fist wrapped around his finger. My heart open and my eyes awake. I was happy, wearing a yellow dress.

Jorge waiting for us on the bench in front of the VA hospital. He was slouched and bored. When he saw the truck, his face came more alive and he rose to his feet quickly, flicking his cigarette. He lifted a white plastic bag that said PATIENT BELONGINGS in large blue letters.

That one time me and Beverly did her aerobics tape together, and I told her that her workout shoes looked like high-tech menstrual pads and she stopped talking to me. She told Jorge about it and instead of scolding me, he laughed, and she got so mad.

Camp

Gold has been found, so the zombies are clapping and bouncing and rollicking with cheer, and they don't care about me. Their eyes are pumice stones, and they drool sebum, but they are happy, they've found gold. Gold gold gold. The most important thing has happened, and that's the most important thing.

A mountain biker, humming, her long blonde hair flapping out behind her helmet, has been batted off her bike and carried, lolling in half, to Mama Cat's dinner table, efficiently dismembered and fed to her mewing babies.

I paw my way through the thick manzanitas, careful not to touch more than necessary. There is no hurry. I do not crush a single silvery leaf with its hopeful new fur. I do not startle any bunnies, do not make them anxious, nor wake any baby rattlesnakes, woven together and resting in a round braid. I do not rouse the Mama Cat who sleeps under the rock and waits for fools like me. I move past her untroubled, untroubling, past the low lake with the heavy wagging stalks surrounding it, and the orphaned yellow paddle from last summer covered now with dark slime, and the clusters of mosquitoes. I am attuned to their tiny needling and swat them quickly, leaving my lower legs spotted with blood, cheetah style. At dusk I fall asleep on a steep slope thick with dry trees, not far from a campfire, I smell the burning wood and burning sugar.

In the morning I wake up to a swarm of voices, excited children. Girls, together, away from home. I hear them dropping down from their bunks and skidding down the dry dirt hill in flopping shoes.

Three-minute showers, girls! comes an adult voice.

I hear the showers going on, the squeals and slams of metal stalls.

Two and a half minutes left, Allie!

Whose shampooooo is this? another girl screams. *Rebecca, is this your shampoooo?*

In my undisturbed area, I rest for three years. I eat the pancakes thrown away by the girls' camp. My only companion during this time is a chocolate brown bull who I can see if I walk to the top of the ridge. I come to know that he is very beautiful.

When I feel I've had enough time in solitude I emerge to seek a different sort of home in the world, also I suspect that I need glasses and I want to see an eye doctor. And I want to try having sex, and also I want candy and other things to eat, I want tampons, books, and other people, possibly friends. But I don't desire any one of these particular things very strongly. Mostly I just want something else.

Two

America's Finest Shitty

A TREMBLING STRIPE OF dark underground civilization quakes just beneath the surface of this sunshine-scrubbed city. Beneath the glittering, garbageless streets is an underbelly family, nightcrawlers, floating eyes, vampires, escapees, undocumented teenagers. I scratched out a niche among them, and lay down in a coffin-shaped room to rest and wait until I know what to do next. I am kept solvent in this static treading by my mother's providence, administered through Roberta, who looks at me with swimmy eyeballs every time I arrive to collect my check. Roberta, good, enduring Roberta, still fiery, still often naked, the bull on her belly warped and blurry now, silver wires sprinkled through her dark curly hair. She is, I suppose, the closest thing I have to a relative. *Do you have an address*, she wants to know. *Are you doing a lot of stimulant drugs*. I know it's love, but I am collapsed to all notions of family and want only to get away from her, from her probing concern. An actual white picket fence surrounds her beach cottage, and I just can't get out of there fast enough, to the other side of that gate. I do appreciate the dribbling money that keeps me safe, enables me to eat food from reliable sources, permits me to help my darker cousins through their constant, colorful financial crises.

There is a bedroom in her house, in Roberta's house, that could be mine if I wanted to stop floating through my 'best years' like a half-deflated balloon, if I wanted to live like a person with a family. I look her deeply in the eyes as she invites me, again, into this life, so that when she reflects later there will be no doubt that I heard and understood and absorbed her offering. A small bedroom painted dusty blue, smelling nice, a grown-up bed with white dressing, a meditation cushion in the corner, a clean window. *Feel into it*. I don't want to feel into it, and I don't want it. Finally she writes me the check and I can leave.

I don't know what you're going through, she says. *I can't imagine. But take with you that I love you. You are loved. Take that with you.*

I do, I say.

Be safe, she says.

I give her a soft hug, and a kiss.

Come to satsang, she says, and I say *not this time*, or *maybe*, or *yes, soon.*

The Pen

I WAKE UP BECAUSE my face is burning because my sunglasses are melting and burning my face. I swat them off and drag a nearby sweatshirt onto my face instead, leaving my mouth uncovered for breathing.

Buggy's face floats into view. Buggy's teeth are gray and brown and come to soft points like candy corns. They are more like teeth-remains than teeth. His lower lip is spotty because he bites it all the time. He's biting it right now. He holds himself curled forward as if holding an invisible ball with his torso, or trying to hide his too-thin body. He is always squinting, and I wonder what he is thinking about or if he needs glasses. He has two shirts. He is glad he found me, wants to bring me to the Pen, to meet Mother and Dooney and everyone else who is the real deal.

Come in, he says, pushing open a door with a hole where the doorknob would be. I follow his bare feet through a sunless room, across a maze of sleeping bodies, a fungus-dark sailor's knot, arms into fabric, feet into armpits. The walls are covered in flyers and remnants of things, spraypainted dots, stickers.

Do all these people live here?

He shrugs and nods in a simultaneous gesture, a whole-body wink. His eyes are shifting all around, he smiles a nervous, churchy smile. He nods toward a translucent plastic city teetering on a wooden windowsill, a sculpture of yellowing tubes, does he have pet rats or something in there? A perfume of desiccated grain and urine lifts from it to my nose.

You have a hamster in there or something?

That's the farm, where I grow the food, he says. *I grow sprouts right here. This thing is a true urban farm. I'm going to patent it.*

He talks to my shoulder. His nose comes to a sharp point and then a little ball.

These are my friends.

He's talking about his fish tank, which is decorated with candy-colored pebbles and some pirate things, but I see no fish.

Fish are shy. This is my studio.

He pushes open a styrofoam door to reveal a broom closet with a child's desk shoved crookedly into it, on this desk is a mess of jars, bottles, brushes, tubes. Covering the side walls of the closet are square wooden panels, a glittering mosaic of minuscule paintings. Each panel depicts a scenario in infinitesimally crisp detail, so much that I have to blink and reorient my eyes many times before reading the images. Trapeze women, clouds with faces, a woman in a skirt that turns into a wedding cake, a cowboy whose forehead has a tiger pushing out of it. There are strokes thinner than hairs, tiny faces with each eyelash and tooth distinct. It takes my breath away.

How do you—

I paint in oils. I use my fingernails. He shakes a glass container of fingernail clippings, some with paint on them, some fresh keratin white. The container was a baby food jar. He holds the fingernail clipping with a pair of tweezers and that's his tool.

A house made of peas and carrots. A monkey wedding, a mountain of books on fire, all in complete, indefatigable detail. It's a lot. Also, it's suddenly warm. And the smell of the oils and chemicals and the overall tart bouquet of the house—feet, scalp, old beans, gloppy furry fish tank. A lot. I press the cool pads of my hands into my eye sockets, black with white possibilities. I see it happen and am powerless to stop it—I divide from my body and clank a few of the panels onto the floor as I pass out and descend like a knocked-over lamp.

I'm sorry, I say first. I was only out for a moment, I think. I don't really know. I've never before fainted. He shrug-winks and laughs. The inside of his mouth is dark and red like a beet. One of the paintings has ended up in my hands.

That was like a movie, I say.

That's my favorite reaction that anybody's ever had.

I've delighted him. The painting I am holding is of a carriage in a field of corn, drawn by rabbits.

I am thinking he will say, *if you like it, keep it.*

I brought you some food, he says instead, and opens his hand to reveal a pile of dry grass that smells like rubber. The smell assaults my nose, moves deep into my brain, waving tickling worms. I fear a re-onset, my knees begin to disappear.

Thank you, no, I still feel . . .

I pull myself up with secret emergency strength and pat my way toward fresh air. There is a girl waking up in the middle of floor, purple acne on her cheeks, I step over her. I unstick the front door and find the street, the already-hot day. The regular world. Across the street there's a little girl in front of an ugly apartment building, wearing a red backpack, kicking the sidewalk. A school bus stops and swallows her gone, leaving a trail of elephant-colored smoke.

I am choosing my life. Is this the life I want?

When I hold the mirror up to my heart, I see a dark circle, feel the single tone of a tuning fork. No answers. Nothing at all to go on. I am a feather in the wind, and when Roberta asks me again, *how does it all make you feel?*, I don't mind the question, I just don't know.

Hot from payday, I buy a dozen fresh bagels and bring them back to the Pen.

Man Made of Wire

BELOW THE PEN, THE man made of wire is continuously cleaning his house, his silvery back bent over, sweeping inside or outside like a never-dying wind-up toy. He repels and hypnotizes me. I do not like to see his body working so hard, dragging a heavy plant, twisting it so the other side now faces the sun. I don't want to see him sucking his powershake through a straw, I do not want to hear about the benefits of injecting vitamins versus swallowing them in a pill, or be introduced to his different muscle groups and invited to touch. I do not want to hear about his past relationships, his next trip, or how when he eats well his poop does not smell offensive, it just smells like the earth. It's difficult to look at his face because it's too active. He is sensitive about it so I try to stare into his eyes and not waver. His eyeballs are surrounded by twisting ropes of silver wire. His teeth are aluminum foil, totally unconvincing.

I fell four stories and lived, he brags.

You know, he says, sweeping invisible dirt, *I never die. I never get depressed. I just keep hustling through the tears.*

The Bath

To meet people is to devour them, to have completed a mission, to move through them.

Rather than friends, I feel like I have a collection. A collection I cherish.

Roberta asks me, *Don't you want to question your assumed outsider status? Why do you just stay there, hovering, wordless? It's like you're not using your life.* I am hardly wordless, I am always making things up. In this way I am a rewriteable slate, a road that's always forking.

'Mother,' a potato-pale woman of indiscernible age and diagnosis, is in the bath with Buggy. She's chewing something, I think uncooked brown rice, and wearing a crumpled hat with her hair all up in it, only a few light strands tickle the back of her neck. I'm sitting on the toilet, clothed, an anthropologist unburdened by tools or methodology. The bathwater is milky gray like mop water. Mother wipes Buggy's eyes and cheeks with a giant sponge. She's one of those women who don't have shoulders, just a steady slope from neck to elbows. The teakettle whistles furiously then gently stops, the door pushes slowly open and a naked boy the color of ivory soap appears, moving slowly, holding the teakettle in front of him like a holy object. Mother and Buggy pull their knees away and he empties the kettle into the tub in a solid steaming stream. This ghostly boy has thick clumpy brown hair that looks like an old woman's wig, and a sweet, tender face with kind dog eyes. He looks about fifteen. I am interested in his genitals, his penis is tiny I think, it doesn't really come out. This is Dooney, he ran away from a religious cult and that's why he's here.

I feel shy so I visit the balcony. Regular people are walking, in pairs and singles, in clean black shoes and sensible pumps. It must be come-home-from-work time. Ladies carry purses and men don't.

The teakettle whistles again and it's me who pours the hot water into the tub this time, more slow and careful than the boy. I want to help.

As she gets out, Mother brushes my arm with her mushy naked breast and leaves an invisible film, a mothprint, she glowers at herself in the mirror as she passes.

The Poetry Doctor

TERRIBLE GOSH!

I will work and save some money, then go to Amsterdam. There is my dream, what's yours? My name is Gypsy and I am nineteen. Okay, really, actually, my name is Benji. My name is Pretty Magic Vanillin Villain, actually.

His name is Alexis and he's getting a Ph.D. in poetry and literature. He will be a poetry doctor. For now, he is just taking a lot of painkillers, lying on the floor of his studio and listening to records, sometimes the same one for two or three days. And sometimes he spins the records manually with one or two fingers, which he is good at doing, he can do it almost 'at speed.' It's meditative, but he shouldn't do it very much because he has bad wrists already, from all the furious, uncontrollable writing, and he never learned to properly hold a pen. He's a real poet. Napkins, toilet paper, whatever. Once he was arrested because he had to write and he didn't have any paper, so he wrote on a lady's car! No, no, that's kind of a myth. He only stole the parking ticket off the car and wrote on *that*. He was reprimanded not arrested. Lately he has been saying the word 'mellifluous' way too much, just *way* too much, he's using it wrong, he's annoying himself. Also he's writing a poem-novel on one long scroll of paper, in homage. Also he is helping his friend build a miniature working volcano in the friend's backyard. So that's what's happening with Alexis.

They died for my sins, he says between cigarette sucks, from his favorite position on the floor, diagonal. *So I can wander through supermarkets at night, bowels buzzing, and feel like I'm part of some kind of respected cultural legacy. You know?*

You're a spy, I say.

Oh my god, he says. *You get it. You're totally my bohemian angel. We are totally Nighthawks at the Diner.*

He must be joking, but then he's not, he is taking himself just as seriously as he can. He's an inflated shirt.

I like the smell of his clothes, cigaretted. I think I may be starting to have boy-girl feelings for him, which I recognize even from this distance as a bad idea.

AT THE COOL COOL party, Alexis sells pills out of a paper bag, a real doctor.

A fine profit, he says sideways. *I paid like twenty-five cents for each of these in Tijuana. At this rate I won't have to take out any more student loans!*

Have some, he says.

Don't want none. Don't like to puke.

You won't puke. Have some, doctor's orders. They're on the house.

I eat two pills, get dizzy then nauseous then tidily throw up in the bushes lining the side of the house. Tidily because I haven't eaten.

The girls here are utter stunners, every one a museum piece, dramatic butterflies with shiny heavy hairstyles and special party outfits. They choke me, stick me to the wall. Here is a light beer to help me feel better. I am transforming into a camera crossed with a flying insect crossed with a molding rug.

My favorite, she's got on a big, dark fur coat and naked legs and little white shoes, I am a hypnotized ape as she comes toward me holding an emptied ashtray. I'm sliding down the wall. My wings are frozen. My throat is filled with cotton and my body is made of clay. Maybe I am overdosing. Her cool doll's hand gently clamps my forearm. I'm possessed by the sweet hardware. I cannot *say something*. She looks into me like looking into a tall glass or a well. I can't speak, because an insect can't speak. I can't speak because we are inside a painting. Her eyebrows are perfect, old-fashioned, designed. Painted. Oh little summertime Mona Lisa!

Let's get you fixed up, okay?

Her voice, girlish and shrill like a lollipop, breaks the love spell somewhat. Her bedroom upstairs, her bedroom, her bedroom, her bedroom, is dark and red and filled with different varieties of smoke, and scarves cover the ceiling in scalloped rows. Her bedroom. The way smoke comes out of a mouth, like soft truck exhaust.

I took pain pills, I say as I lie down on her bed, a pulsing cloud. *Normally I'm much more personable.* There's a small, heavy euphoria in my pelvis. She's brushing through some drawers, her fingernails scratching the wood. She pulls up a black dress with a bow around the neck.

Pretty, I say.

Try it on. You'll feel better.

Who, me? I look around for a place to get undressed. *Just take it off, girl*, she says. Girl! I remove my CORONA sweatshirt, a pair of once-black stretch pants and army surplus combat boots, I manage it without falling over although my body is shifting like slippery plates. Standing there in my sports bra and dismal yellow panties, I feel my body glowing like a bulb. If it's shame, it is a luminous kind of shame. I don't mind it. She arranges me into the dress, her officious hands assuring with their brief, tacky touches that there is nothing whatsoever flirtatious happening here.

She scooches me in front of the mirror. I see a tall man with hairy legs wearing a dress, the stomach overfilled.

See? Told you, she says. *I'm too short for that dress, but it looks good on you. How tall are you?*

I don't know.

What size shoe are you?

Ten I think. In women's.

She gets on all fours, swipes beneath the bed with a metal hanger, hooking something. She presents to me a pair of dusty silver shoes, flattened like they'd been run over by a car. She pops them skillfully back up into 3-D.

They won't fit, I say.

Try them.

I work them onto my feet. They fit okay but the heels are tall and taper to a pencil-eraser-size contact with the earth, a foolish design.

She smooths my hair down against my skull and pulls my sideburns, waxing them into coquette curls. She smears my eyebrows with spit-damp fingers. It feels so good. Her spit smells salty. I want her to slip her fingers into my skull and live there forever, sweet octopi.

I'm sorry I'm dirty, I say. *I'm kind of a gypsy.*

Such good skin, she says to my shoulder. It's like she's dealing with my body without me in it.

Her hair is blonde and pulled up tight and is a pearl, in color and sheen, and radiates.

She puts lipstick on her finger, *I do it better when it's on my finger,* and smears it on my lips. It tastes like . . .

Stop licking it.

My knees are ancient gray stone, my leg hair a humiliation. My body ruins it.

I'm embarrassed about my leg hair, I say. *It kind of clashes with the . . .*

She gives me some black tights that itch but I should just give them a try. Just try, just try.

THE STREETLIGHTS HAVE THICK halos tonight. A dense layer of white noise frosts every exchange and leaves ghost icicles. But it's not cold, that's not what I mean. I'm in a canoe, bobbing in a thick indigo river, inside a fairytale village in sweet kodachrome miniature. A little house, a child's house, around the bend. I plop my oar in the water and endeavor to steer toward it. The windows glow out saffron. Cinnamon perfumes the air. The water is thick, like black oil. I am inside a warm book. I hear the pages turn. The moon is a glowing tooth. The moon is watching. The moon is a woman. I want to embody this girl who's in my little boat with me, whose name is Anna, who radiates. Anna Hosanna. My new personal stylist. My new tender. I want my arms inside her arms. My bones in her bones, to be a secret stowaway just for a moment. Just for a few breaths. Just an experiment. I follow her like a baby duck, she doesn't mind, she's helping the new girl. The new girl is breathing in her hair. She moves like an efficient insect, greeting everyone, kissing the girls, the catalogue of girls, the wind turns the pages of the catalogue of the girls. The magnitude of beauty seems absurd, a crashing flood of wealth, a mountain-size altar of gleaming opulent riches. The new tide washes up scores of fresh beauties daily. Your mouth is always full. How many lovely girls does one globe need? How is it possible, this bottomless honey pot of love, fresh bewitchment shooting from heart to heart like a constant storm of comets, currency printed without tracking numbers, without limit, raining all the time? Impossible, yet here we are. Every woman a new flavor of alluring, a new, unique orgasmic melody. It fills me with fucking magnetic fucking sand. I like it in the soft dark bedroom, where the girls come to check their make-up and do drugs, touching each other's waists and dealing compliments fast and loose like glossy new playing cards, I like the sound of her hands clicking through things inside her purse, coming up with her silver cigarette case, finding the glass vial of cocaine and tap tapping it out with her little finger. I am a blob of dough with giant eyes pinned open, a toy on a chair.

Alexis the poetry doctor is looking for me, he wants me next to him, he wants a dedicated chuckling witness to his incessant chronicling, a sidekick, an audience. I feel him sucking around for me like a sea creature.

Remember me? he says, poking his head in the bedroom door. *I brought you to this party? Hey, nice dress!*

At the party women come and go, looking for someplace to snort their blow, he professes, as I pinch the door shut on his face.

Girls only!

THE SOUND IS LOTS of popcorn kernels popping. It's loud. I pull on the helmet and climb onto the rear of the seat, pulling up the black dress nearly to my hip bones so I can open my legs enough to straddle.

Hold on tight, Anna says. *Are you going to throw up again?*

I don't think so, I say, but I don't know what is happening.

I put my hands on her hips. I don't want to do anything weird.

Hold on tight, she says. *Don't be shy. Put your arms around me. Just grab me.*

If you have to throw up just tell me, she says.

The back brake doesn't really work, she says.

My arms are around her tight. We're one thing.

In her belly the rattler's rattle. Her belly is soft like dough.

She pops it into gear and we jolt forth, strong vibrations are broadcast throughout my body. Just grab me.

The Zoo

An ice sculpture. An ice swan. We two supermodels. I am a woman. I am seriously a woman, look at my silver decoration shoes, my tender corners and my architect-angle corners. A design to be beheld, I'm even wearing a bow. The scooter is also womanly. We climb off it. I learn to walk again.

The flamingos are deep-sleeping, maybe dreaming, maybe frozen. Even when they pat and bend they are waking-sleeping. I'd like to wrap a ribbon around each impossible neck, for decoration. Instead of a Christmas tree I'd like to have just a few flamingos in the living room. The ponds are as still as glass. Cavities in the walls of the man-made rock. Cuteness is the currency here. Cuteness unplugged. All the guards are sleeping, the double decker buses are sleeping, the soft-serve ice cream machines are humming in their sleep, resting up for tomorrow, the highwire cable cars, aka 'Skyfari' are also at rest. The snakes are coiled up and warm behind thick glass. Warm reptile drool comes out of their mouths, a delicacy.

I am content to appreciate the scene from without, but my companion, my *companion*, insists it's time to climb the fence. Oh, *genial*, as Alexis says. Poor Alexis, where is he? Sniffling into his cash wad? I am ready for whatever. The pointed silver toes are actually practical now, they make easy work of the chain-link fence and I am a human elevator, half goat. At the tippy top, I pause to behold the landscape, one leg on either side of the rippling fence, reaping full benefits of my uncommon stature. I enjoy the dark tableau, the world inside out. I know I should keep three points on the fence at all times and I do. No more dying!

Chita! Anna hisses up at me, her blonde helmet a terrestrial beacon in the smeared starry night. Smeared and drifting. Oh, the cosmos in my belly. Oh, her shoulders, tense from anxiety.

Hi, I say. *You look nice*. She's nervous, watching me teeter up there. But I am not worried. This is a good place to be, you can feel so much and understand so much from up here. How wildness is combed into pleasure. The excrement of family fun, the depressed shadows of the large dark animals moving slowly, the piles of shining black garbage bags. The world underneath the world, worms and slugs under the iceplant, the dirt is alive, the walkways tiled with green glass and turquoise sparkle and flirt just a little bit. Teeth, fingers, slime, fingernails. Men engineered and sculpted this whole thing—I mean not just the zoo but the WHOLE THING—out of only a few basic humors. Apartment buildings new and large, lining each hill on the distant horizon, impacted teeth. Fabricated from petrified cake, sprayed with lacquer so they will not dissolve in the first rainstorm, but will withstand a year or two. Senior Living San Diego–Style, Units Available Now—the pink-and-green sign glows crisply for all the restless seniors wandering the streets in the middle of the night, considering their next move. And me, I am a lone barnacle. A slightly dizzy barnacle, drunk on salt. Hanging on by my soft teeth. A giant tree, as still as a stone, with beckoning fingers instead of leaves. Whistling Spanish castles with red tile roofs. What's in all the dark passageways? Men with beards, wild eyes, shining knives. Smoking something? Something something? Something in the pants. Something swaying and curling and having thoughts of its own. Men of the hill, the canyon, the bush. Men of the rat, rat hunters, rat on a stick cookers, wiping their asses with a leaf. Not wiping their asses at all, what does it matter? Grooming is for kings and queens. Ghosts come in different flavors. Ghosts fuck other ghosts to create infant ghosts, who do not cry when they're born. El Cid is out there too, striking a pose. Children are curled, sleeping in the giant fig tree, making it breathe, making it creep even bigger, very slowly, but I can see it move, expand. That tree is as big as a city. Children hold on to each other, brother and sister, cousin and cousin. Holding chilly hands involuntarily in sleep, a chain of flesh and bone, braiding together naturally. Bone-deep in the tree they sleep, in slits and baby burrows, and disappear each morning like dew. Little gypsies everywhere. If I choose to look, I see . . .

Come ON!, Anna hisses at me hard from the ground. *What the fuck! Go OVER!*

The death impulse bubbles up in me without warning, a real surprise. Its big easy hands fitting all the way around my neck so clean. It's not passionate, not a siren's tempting song, just a clear option. Take your place on the family tree, walk on the blackened, crispy branch, bring us a tray of tea. It would be fast. It would be easy. The tree grows underground, unrolling darkly, wetly. The next place. A natural progression to the next place. But don't I like this place? This one right here? I like Anna, with her arms on her hips in frustration, her fists as pretty as Christmas tree bulbs.

Get the fuck over!, she calls up. She is really wanting to get the highwire portion of this adventure over with, that's reasonable. Totally respect that. I move my leg over, behind me, the fence shimmies and my leg sticks there, a frozen figure skater. Three points. Look, see, I don't want to die after all. Look how my body clings to life. This is my body's nature. Getting down was harder than getting up but finally I arrive at the ground and from there I can see how tall the fence was. I really could have died, but there will be other opportunities.

Anna begins her climb, loses a shoe, goes back down to get it and starts again. She gets high up, her white panties glowing like the moon. *Thuck!* goes her weight on the asphalt when she hops down.

She stands with her legs apart, her toes pointing out, arms crossed, a superhero's stance, claiming our land.

KAIA TOOK ME TO the zoo all the time when I was a kid. So often that some of the animals felt like friends, and I knew the whole layout. I hadn't thought about it in so long, but now the memory comes back clearly, as waves of familiar smells hit me, animal shit and sour grain and dulcet hay.

In the nursery, on the other side of the glass, a baby monkey sleeps, like a cheesecake starlet with his diapered butt up in the air, clutching a blanket to his face. His diaper's loose and I can see the beginning of his little butt, a tender cleft peach. His pink skin is covered in hair, his ears are huge.

Name: Harry, species: chimpanzee, age: 6 weeks, health: good. His back rises and sinks, teaspoons of breath. Above him hangs a tangle of red and yellow plastic chains, for playing.

Let's kidnap her, says Anna, pointing to a brown piglet asleep in the incubator in the next window. The piglet is as big as a human infant. It has veins.

Beverly. 25 days old. Born premature. Health: Fair. Jaundiced.

THE PETTING ZOO, MY sunshiney toddler haunt, is now eerie and lifeless. The gate is open, gently bobbing, sprinkled straws of hay on the ground are moved now and then by the wind's fingers.

There's still the table where children can touch and even pick up tiny chicks. A memory grips me suddenly and makes me urgently sad, like it's happening right this moment. I was eight or nine. A small boy, older than me but still small, had picked up a teeny bird and squeezed. I could have done something but I just watched. I was trying to *edit my desire* for *control*. The bird was desperate and helpless in the fist, looking around, peeping and trying to kick her way out but also resigned and trusting and just tiny, so tiny and moist lemony yellow. The boy's mother, who had not been paying attention, turned around and saw what was happening and seized the boy's fist and gasped, and the boy began to cry of course and of course the bird was dead, and a worker took the lifeless bird away. The boy's mother was enraged, yelling at the boy in a language that was not Spanish or English, yelling with big gestures and the boy was choked quiet, dark, traumatized. Maybe he's in therapy now. Maybe he's a buyer of self-help books. He's probably a violent criminal now, licking his knives.

ICE CREAM TIME! WE pull the industrial lever together, our four hands making a mountain of hands, a multitude of fingers. The substance leaps out of the machine, an eager extrusion of snowy white. Anna squats and puts her mouth on the nozzle and I pull the lever slowly, filling her throat. She swallows it and licks the drops off her hands, then moves over and it's my turn so I squat and arrange the thing into my mouth and she pulls the lever for me. The icy stuff pushes into me, around my teeth, down the hatch, filling my belly like a balloon, stretching. I frost my lips with it. I carry away a handful, licking as I walk, dripping down Anna's poor pretty dress.

We are walking down the wide ramp toward the Reptile Kingdom when I feel it coming, an insistent seismic correction. I greet it with hospitality, I puke up the ice cream, arcing twisting fireworks of white onto the blacktop. Fresh and fun. When I finish, I stumble backward and admire my work. My jaws are still watering, my knees are scraped. Sweet candy teeth. The puke looks like the shit splatters of a great beast from another age, dropped from miles above. The milky way.

I'm high, she says and reaches out for my hands. Her eyes are candles floating in a bowl. I accept her hands, we naturally clasp. And this way we form an invincible power, something from the very old world, from the very old book, from a myth.

Me too, I say. *I'm sorry about your dress.*

Our shoulders come together like pages in a book. My hands are oddly sensitive to her touch, they've been peeled open. Her kisses on my cheek make the sound of a needle pricking fabric. I reach for her throat and she drops to the ground in dramatic consent, or unconsciousness. It's consent, so I wrap my arms around her neck and begin my embodiment through her seashell neck, swallowing up her spine. Our bones fuse together, we become one weight, we roll into the ratty brush, we hold on tight and I eat her neck with my new teeth. I wake up as dawn cracks with her pearls in my mouth, and empty, and hungry. I want all her parts, we've only just begun.

Nutritional Information

Have something substantive, I say to Buggy. *Let me buy you a protein smoothie.*

Boogers are part of the food chain, he says. *It's an adaptation.*

I'm totally out of the closet about eating my boogers, he says, nibbling at his thumbnail.

I shit at least twice a day, he says. *That's how much people should shit. At least.*

My father was a doctor, Buggy says. *He got all the pills he wanted.*

My mother was a guru, I say. *I got all the sugar I wanted.*

Wish

Lately I do not sleep. Why? Because I am a supernatural creature who does not need sleep like these skin-covered mortals? Silly waterbugs?

Everyone else sleeps, Mother P sleeps, sitting up against the wall, as if awake and watching us, but I'm sure she's sleeping because she's snoring. She's got a new necklace on, a large crystal and a fork, and she's wearing that deflated scrotum of a hat like always. Maybe she'll be mad at me, maybe she won't care. Maybe she is just joking when she says 'do not touch the Little Boys, only bad people touch my Little Boys,' et cetera. It's a concern because following the prelingual directives of the girl-boy book of things that just happen, Dooney, with whom I am sharing the big chair, who'd been napping, sweetly nestled against me, has woken up, found my tits and is squeezing them and I don't feel like saying no, though I don't particularly feel like yes either. He is touching me, I'm not touching him, so maybe it's allowed. And Dooney's pretty, his lips are soft as scallops, there is something precious as he kisses me and he tastes clean, surprisingly clean like a baby, and it feels very innocent. He advances clumsily, a shaky adolescent pendulum with its inevitable course, the simplest machine. Unless deterred, the boy will find the breasts. The boy will unearth the pussy. The boy will deal with the pussy. Even this boy, this tender, shuffling, traumatized boy. The rules still apply. The apple will hit the ground. I am thinking about stopping him, I could make him stop, I don't really want it, I feel like I might fart, and we're right here with other people and it makes me shy, or it makes me *embarrassed*. I could say *stop*, but I don't say stop. It goes and goes. He is less shy. He is not really shy at all. He lies on top of me and his weight is good, he sucks my tits, it feels pretty good but I can't look, and I don't want him to look either, I cover his eyes. He wants my pants off, he wants it so bad I want him to have it, too. Ultimately he holds my legs open, I feel splayed and silly like a broken wishbone, he opens my pussy with his hands and licks me softly, making out with it. It's making me hard but I am also sort of disgusted and I want it faster and I also don't want it, now he has a puppyish excitement and my ambivalence falls over into an involuntary, pukey feverish climax which makes me want to yell and thrash but I stay quiet, so quiet, I just hold my own hands over my belly so hard, and I'm glad it's over and I feel that something medical has happened.

You're beautiful, he whispers, his chin shiny with my slime. *Do you mind if I masturbate?*

It's your house, I say. *Go for it.*

Well, it's everyone's house I guess. All are welcome to masturbate here. You don't even have to ask. I put my pants on, my pussy readjusting to things. While Dooney jacks himself I enjoy the fuzzy blips of lights shooting around the walls, the cars' passing headlights being tossed around. Dooney is breathing fast and hard and finally finishes, wipes the jizz off his stomach with a once-white sock from the floor then throws it back. It smells like our mix of genitals and I hope by morning it mixes in with the other funks and becomes undiscernible and I hope I have not soaked the chair with my come, I don't want to have to look at my come on this chair every time I'm here forever and remember this weird thing. Soon Dooney is asleep again (baby) and he doesn't rouse when I lift his heavy arms and extricate myself, dizzily putting on my shoes (no socks), trundling toward the door greasy-limbed.

I close the door quietly, don't wake the moldy babies, their chests rising and falling together, their grim expressions and tangled hair. Poor babies, menagerie of recklessness, baring teeth, bearing nightmares, take care little ones.

I go to the beach and stay for a while.

Beloved

SHE'S FOUND LOVE, SO could I lend her some money? She has never asked before. This is not exactly true. I mean she does not ask but she says, *Oh, how many donuts did you get?* Anyway yes I can give you some money. Loan you some money.

But first I will hear all about it. They are so in love they're like two hands pressed together in prayer. They are two wheels on the same bicycle on a hot black road. They will be married! Marriage, the happiest day of a woman's life! They met in the canyon a long time ago, but just recently realized they are each other's destiny. His name is Dean Jean, a sacred rock collector, rugged cowboy-boot wearer, snake killer, snake eater. He's off to Arizona now, getting his horse back, picking dirt out of the horse's feet, getting everything ready, taking naps on rocks. Soon Mother P will pack up her things and meet him there, and they will live with his unpredictable but ultimately very loyal dog Spit, in a trailer against the turquoise sky, she will sew curtains, add a woman's touch. She can't leave right now because of that whole mix-up with the checking account and the traveler's checks. When you're down, it's easy to go downer. System's set up like that.

And here's a big thing—she will get her kid back—her real kid, her real blue-eyed boy, nine years old, or ten now actually. She just has to get the ball rolling. She just has to stand up straight.

This isn't me, you know, she says, swinging her hand to describe the whole world. *This is just a phase. I'm actually a very competent person. Did you know I was a physician?*

Being a bald woman in America, it's hard, she says. *I wouldn't wish it on anyone. Anyone.*

Don't you want to see? she asks.

Of course I do. She pulls off her hat. She's not bald, it's just a little thinner on top. If she parted it on the side it wouldn't be noticeable. It's really not bad, I offer.

Do you think it helps if you say that? You don't have a clue!

Normal Sex

I ASCEND A HAUNTED STAIRCASE lit by one dangling blue bulb.

Go ahead, he says. *No one's home.*

It's not true. Dostoyevsky is glowering at us from the top of the stairs, holding his pants closed, barely.

On my host's bed is a family of modified dolls. A giant blue rabbit has four ears and a third googling eye and soft dangling chutes of rubber genitalia. A green parrot has goat hooves and a rosary around her neck. My host has a nice profile, pleasant and clean. On the inside of both wrists are tattoos of crossed swords which are so new they seem fake.

I'm not supposed to scratch my new tats, he says. *But I've always scratched my wrists, just a habit. I think I keep a lot of energy right there.*

I see. He is wearing nice shoes that are like shiny black canoes. He removes them with delectation. I wonder if in the history of the world a scientist has ever fallen in love with an unconscious research subject. The answer must be yes.

We lie down, the bed sinks and pulls us together in the middle, another character in the story, the inevitable story. A bathtub full of blood. What is about to happen.

He tugs at a clump of hair above my ear. The animals get pushed off the bed. Animals were pushed off the bed in the making of this film. A teddy bear with turtle claws, six eyes and a sewn-on smirk. Two green leather mice. His cold finger in my ear. He puts four fingers in my mouth.

Suck hard, he says, but I can't close my mouth around so many fingers and I push his wrist away. A lot of energy there. Maybe I can't do this after all? Maybe I actually do not want to. I just feel like I have to because I need to understand this thing that everyone else is so into. But maybe I can't? He massages my crotch softly with one hand like chewing gum in slow motion, unfolding my resistance like a cloth napkin. I think I can latch on to this machine now. I let him take off my clothes because this is actually going to happen. I even help out. This is serious, the ancient book creaking open, the ancient syllabary swirling around our skulls. I must not laugh and shatter the flimsy theater, must not pull away the curtain. His synthetic fabrics are vivid against my back, impressing their texture. He rubs my belly and chest and face slowly, like frosting a cake, like a clairvoyant. Me, naked with a man. I do not laugh. The force that makes the world spin is right in your two hands, young woman. In opposition to his dark need I am female, the relenter, the desired and the decider. Instructions whispered from the booth. Open your throat. Touch yourself. Don't be shy. Enjoy yourself. Let it happen. Don't laugh. I'm going to say yes. It's fun, actually.

Can I fuck you? he asks, the eyes of a rodent in a trap. A good little face. Sure you can! Isn't that what we came to do? His hands quiver as they open the bedside drawer, the ballet continues. This is what people do! I am people!

Slowly and with tenderness, even maybe affection, he changes my geography to suit his desire, his body pressing into mine, finally entering sharply. The eros crumbles away in fast motion. The motion is dumb, too simple and it doesn't feel right. I think I understand feminism now. How long will it last? I can't find that part of the instructions. I am flipping through. I am not included.

You look good, he says. *You look good when I'm fucking you.*

I like it, I say for him and the secret audience, and it is true, in a conceptual way, in an aspirational way, but something feels like it's going wrong.

I still have hope for a good finish. I touch myself and that makes it better. He has his orgasm, holding onto my hair and gurgling into my neck as his trunkette pulses out its final expression. I let it fall out and wiggle around to arrange myself so I won't have contact with any seepage. I feel my pussy with my fingers.

It's the same, but different, a real hole pressed open! This legend is real! You can put a thing in it. A sizable thing. A pair of glasses. A small bottle of shampoo.

Everything okay down there? he says.

I have a hole in my body, I say.

How many orgasms did you have? he says.

Um, none.

He presses his knuckles softly into my face. We're buddies.

Did you say none or nine?

Can I lick you? he asks. *I wanna make you come.* I don't think I'll come, it's too bright, but he doesn't wait for the answer and I just let him do whatever, he's into the hole. I imagine the possibilities for experimentation, the bright future of this hole. Now I want him to stop. He doesn't stop. *Nothing in the hole*, I demand. The struggle itself is where the romance lies. I have a lot to think about. I come, finally, my body's way of saying, *okay, jeez*.

On my way out I touch his tidy belt collection hanging on the wall, they move like wind chimes. I pull the bookmark from his book as a trick.

Shaking. The hole broke bright and alive. A neon sign shines into a warbling greasy puddle. The air is stagnant, a stage set. There on the corner a woman is drunk, heavy, leaning into her man. I know about them now because I've done it myself. He squeezes her waist.

Uncovered, excavated, each cell in my body scrubbed and shining and singing. Dirt turned over, all the little tender critters upended and shrinking from the sunlight. I'm the same person, picked up and shifted over a few inches. I didn't really like it, but I liked learning how bodies can change together, how different your body can be from one hour to the next.

I just had sex, I say secretly, my teeth clenched like a ventriloquist. *Sex sex sex*. I say it to the fence I'm walking by, I say it to that car. I've heard the rattler's rattle. I've had the *snake in my mouth*. I wish I had someone to tell who would care a little.

Did I just fall in love? I hope not. Maybe my body fell in love a little bit, it's shaking and wants a long hug. His name was Ketchup. I will always remember that name so I'm glad it's a pretty good one.

Confession

THE COVER OF KAIA'S *third* posthumous book is a picture of her at a public appearance shaking a lady's hand. They've doctored the photograph and Kaia looks flawless, waving like a beauty queen with a sharp gleam in her eye. Under her chin it reads, *Lasting Gifts: Notes From a Life Well-Lived*. Roberta's house is full of boxes of these books, boxes climbing up the walls.

Is it any good? I ask, leafing through.

Of course, she says. *There's a picture with you in it.* She opens the book, looking for it, but I don't care about it.

I take the check, folded in half. I care about that. Fund of the Decrepits.

As I'm walking out the door, I'm overcome. I have to tell someone who cares.

I had sex with a boy! We had intercourse!

She looks puzzled. *You hadn't already?*

No way.

Wow. I assumed . . .

What? I say.

Honestly?

Yeah.

Well, one that you're kind of a lesbian? Type of thing? And two, just that you'd have already tried all that?

Lesbian. That was not a word I liked. Typewriter, moustache. Lesbian. Lesbian. I liked it a little bit more and a little bit more. But still not much. Tennis ball. Knee. Fiber.

Season's Greetings

THE FOG FALLS IN!

Smears a sad beachy feeling all over the city. Throws its holy water all over everything. The beach in wartime, still and joyless, vintage naval grey, the only visible life is heavy birds moving like slowly spinning records. Foraging petrified french fries or ketchup-soaked paper plates, better than nothing! Where normally the sun blowtorches down and melts people like butter it is now prickly cool, melancholy, thin blood. The weather has stepped in with her military shoes to ensure we won't forget her altogether. That we won't forget that there is such a thing as weather.

The fog spills between the buildings like milk into tea. Thick enough that my ankles look soft and my (lesbian) toes are barely visible.

My exhaust-o-vision I suppose compounds the impact of this weird weather event. An invisible belt prohibits correct breath and everything has a buzzing edge. I'm enforcing my strategy, I will walk all day, in hopes that it will make me sleep at night. I've fallen once so far, I banged my wrist on a car's mirror while I was tumbling but I'm okay, just a little blood, just a scratch, just a little dizzy, just haven't been sleeping. I'm a pigeon.

A lady had asked me if I was okay and I'd waved.

Around the majestic fish pond with fairytale lily pads I walk and walk. I imagine falling in like a pebble, drowning wordlessly, open mouthed, water filling me up, my eyes open all the time, as noncombative as an infant. Surrender, lie down on the tracks, invite harm. (Lesbian) corpse pose. Unzip everything, go without a wink or a sound loud enough to cut the air. The possibility of disappearance is a dissolving pill, a shred of cotton candy melting to nothing in my wet fingertips before I can bring it to my mouth. My little scrape could go either way, it could heal itself or it could unheal, the fissure splitting like a faultline. I'm ready to rot.

What is a lifetime? I will decide what is my lifetime. I might go to Roberta's peaceful blue bedroom, change into good clean clothes tonight. Go to sleep, my very own sleep where I will actually rest and dream my own puffy cottony dreams. The ghosts looking in the windows, licking their lips at me. Fucking assholes. Fuck you. I am having some seriously deep thoughts here. Everything would be okay if I could sleep like other people. Then I would not be secretly drowning all the time.

But I don't actually feel depressed. I mean, I don't think I would use that word. Roberta looked at me with such pity in her eyes, like I'm so wanting. But I feel very much nothing. She wants me to come to satsang, to sit and chant with them. Everyone wants to see me. Don't I want to see them?

It's safe to say I don't.

Namaste, she says as I leave, fluttering check in hand.

I pretend I did not hear. I don't want to say fucking *namaste*.

Was it a joke, had Roberta said that there is a Kaia-branded vitamin line in the works? Well maybe I would get millions of dollars from it, a pyramid scheme pumping blood right to my heart. And I would funnel the money right to the kids at the Pen.

What if we all had money? I think we'd be really sharp dressers.

Hazard Cone

I JUST BONED THAT girl, says Ketchup, my sexual partner, the one with the dick. *She's super fun.*

The "girl" he is referring to is walking down the street and is as tall as a skyscraper. She is beyond beauty, she's overshot it, and now resides squarely in the territory of insect robot sex machine, her short blocky hair is hazard-cone orange as she spiders along with a slick shopping bag. She opens the door to a cute old car, slips into it like an eel, presses on enormous black sunglasses and putters off. I want to catch her face but I only see her papery jaw pounding chewing gum then the blackened window-size glasses, looking over her shoulder, switching lanes then she's gone. We are watching her from the Pen balcony, spying, Ketchup is smoking a handrolled cigarette. His eyes aren't looking at me but I can tell there is a lively little mischief in them which I think is because he is delighted in seeing that he has made me a tiny bit, maybe, something like, maybe a little bit jealous. He still thinks about me when he jacks off et cetera. He doesn't see why we don't sleep together again. Because *we already did*, I say again, and he tells me I am cruel, but I am not cruel, I am made of pencils, and plus I am gay or asexual or unfeeling or whatever. I never mention that he was my first and so far only experiment of the penetrative nature. I keep that little locket in my blouse. And now he's got a girl anyway, with magazine-perfect punk rock hair and they must look so good together.

STAR! Donuts

I AM ENJOYING A basket of donut holes and considering onion rings for dessert. I peel the red seal off the bottle of orange juice.

Mother P comes in from the closet of night, glowing like a bone, trudging like a sleepwalker. Her feet do not lift as she moves, her legs do not bend, she scrapes along in tiny increments, her mouth open as if singing one continuous note. That *darn hat* again like a paper bag smashed on her skull. She trips and only her legs respond, catching her, her upper body stays still. When she is imminently proximate she shudders awake. Up close she is a zombie held together with scotch tape. Even her eyes are taped open. Her face is a sleepless froggy mask.

Using hand signals I offer to buy her: Coffee? Food? You want something?

She physically agrees.

The worker stops sweeping to hand her a basket of three donuts.

She sits across from me with her basket of donuts, but doesn't look at me. She's burrowing into the icing. She's got chocolate sprinkles like mouse turds all over her lips.

Are you alright, Mother? I ask. No reply. A different angle:

You been okay? Nobody's seen you in like three days.

We got married, she says. *Dean Jean married me in a magical cactus forest.*

She taps herself on the shoulder.

Arizona. Sunburn, she says.

She holds up her hand and there is a thin gold band. Her fingernails are gnawed down to nothing, raw finger flesh puffing up around the tiny traumatized shells of nails.

Wow! Congratulations! How was the wedding?

Small. When she speaks, crumbs fly.

Who was there? I say.

Who was there? she repeats back.

I mean, was it his family, your family, who?

Oh. Not family really. Just friends. A few friends. His dog. Spiritual Dog. His dog Spit.

Was it nice? Was there a cake?

Mother P is picking a sprinkle out from inside her shirt. Her breathing is getting harder. What is her prob.

You okay? I ask.

Wah! she cries suddenly, and bounces up as if someone has stepped on her tail, then sits back down. *I hate lying! I can't deal with lying. I wasn't in Arizona. We didn't get married in Arizona, okay! We got married in prison. Dean Jean is in prison. I took the bus and we got married in prison.*

Wow!

Shit. Fuck. Now he's going to kill me.

She covers her two eyes with her two hands.

He told me if I told anyone, the dog would eat me.

She dumps her face into the donut basket, now empty. A splatter of crumbs.

The Piñata

Some evictions happened, so things rearrange, Ketchup moved in with his new girlfriend with the hazard-cone hair who is called 'Sarah'—she *would* be called Sarah—and her tiny black dog called Minuet with a darling cocked, smashed-up face and thumb-size bubblegum-pink tongue. Alexis the poetry doctor, and Anna Hosanna my glowing girl, live there, too. It's a real house with a front yard and a bench on a little concrete porch. We are spraypainting vertical gold stripes onto the walls, using masking tape as guides, I am helping, Ketchup is making vegan something in the kitchen.

So this guy shows up on a bicycle, this big-jawed, shuffly, creamy-brown coolio boy in a square hunting jacket, and he turns out to be Anna's new boyfriend, I mean not her boyfriend but the boy she *is seeing*, a "drummer" called Marco. I had thought that the others, like me, were too cool for coupling, but it's taken hold, it's spreading like a nasty disease, everyone falling into everyone's arms, suddenly buying birthday presents and cutting vegetables together. I'd told Anna I'd take the pictures for her new band 'Cassingle' but I didn't know it was her plus this dude. To refuse based on that seems dorky so I'll just grind through. She and the beau nouveau giggle like drunk retards, throw made-up gang signs. He's putting his hands all over Anna's waist very casually, around her neck so casually. They are like Siamese twins, they require no personal space, nothing is off limits, they'd swallow each other's heads if they could. I'm more and more delicately nauseous. Flash, whine, flash, whine. I won't throw up, that's only my mind's trick, and my mind does not control me. She knows which is the good side of her face, she knows what colors suit her. She snuggles in his jacket like a marsupial. It fits around her, it fits around them both, how cute that she's nestled like an animal against its mama dada. You shouldn't barf at love, love is real. Chocolate syrup stands in for blood as they gleefully perform violence, smears of darkness on his cheeks, both pairs of eyes rolled up as in spirit possession, two pretty, possessed faces, happy death. This roll of film is black and white so the chocolate can be blood.

I follow Anna into the bathroom, she got some chocolate in her eye. I am having the weirdest feeling, the nausea and something that must be envy, a kind of angry violent disgust and dismissal, I want to tell her goodbye because she's a boy's marsupial clutch and that's nasty and I don't even want her anymore, but then there is her swan-white neck, and her little elfy ear that my tongue wants to enclose and eat.

Don't freak out on me, Chita, Anna says, looking over at me while rubbing her eye. *He's just a boy.*

She kisses me softly on the mouth, and my heart rolls out the bottom of my stomach but our kiss is dry like a paper envelope.

Anna and Marco are *without shirts* now, pretending to be gouging out each others eyes with plastic spoons. This one is for the back of the single. They'll be clothed and loving on the front, then hateful and murderous and naked on the back. Too clever. I'm only shooting from the neck up. He's adopted a new expression, he's found his 'surprised' face. He's not so bad. He works as a security guard at Vons. On his break he smokes out by the recycling domes and eats the thrown-away expired food so he can spend all his money on records. He would be fun to swing on a branch with. Naked Jesus. He would be fun to dance with, dumb monkey ass monkey. I don't vomit and I don't run away, and the old world just goes on spinning.

Ketchup carries a cocktail tray, but not with cocktails, with white powder drugs on one third and mushrooms on one third and then Runts on the other third. Runts the candy. Like a sinewy snake he slithers up to a person and puts things on their tongue, jester shaman pharmacist conductor of mood, feather twirler, nipple tickler. He thinks he's so handsome. Did you know that everyone hates banana-flavored Runts? Nobody wants them except maybe some dumb kindergarteners or babies who don't know anything, or dogs. But we can't give Minuet any food, he has special dietary needs. Thus banana Runts pile up on the tray. I was not interested in drugs but my mouth opened and closed and they are being ingested just like that and they taste *nasty*.

We must practice various forms of dance that involve moving in a line, such as moonwalking. It's hard to do on carpet so the bench is taken from the porch—by whom, it doesn't matter, we're all the cosmic same—we take it apart and put down the plank of wood but it's actually no better than carpet in terms of moonwalking on it so we get it wet and it still doesn't work, so Marco has an idea and he sprays it with Pam until it gleams and he can moonwalk so good now, he can levitate. We're all delighted but then Sarah freaks out. She thinks Minuet might be allergic to aerosol products because he's being spacey, she thinks, Marco calls that a *buzzkill*, but really no one wants to hurt little Minuet and so Ketchup heroically pitches the plank onto the front lawn, it lands with flecks of Pam like spittle still sizzling, and we eschew moonwalking practice for now. That's okay. Sarah collects Minuet in her skinny pipey arms and holds him, walking around the house with her orange head talking straight into his sponge-head. Minuet is fine, his black face looks like it was smashed by a truck like usual but he is beautiful besides that, and alive, his little pink tongue is alive.

The rodent in my chest is running much too fast. I drink some smoky darkness which peels layers off my throat as it washes down. The liquid speaks to other liquids in a network of secret speakers, a pinball machine jockeying the 'invisible vibrations.' A too-big piece of ice slides down my throat perfectly.

People think invisible vibrations are so far out, right?, begins Alexis the poetry doctor as he paces the lawn holding his silly flask, aping a preacher. *And I'll say, well, do you believe in sound? Are you hearing me right now? Because do you know what sound is? Sound is ex-actly invisible vibrations. And then they stop and think.*

I'm not a total fruitcake, he says. *Science is on my side.*

I am incorrigibly in love with you, he says. *Be mine.*

I don't know if he even knows who he's talking to. Yes, his eyes are sliding down his face with LOVE, but he's looking through me, also I think he just wanted to say 'incorrigibly.' It's all a messy tray of brownies, muddy bootprints, a twisty window. His hand definite-ly around my throat. This crude language absolves the gravity, in-vites a wave of mud. We don't know. I guess we could do it. Here's something I know, I can see his twin nipples beneath his filmy yellow blouse and am repelled at a gut level. Now I have Alexis the poetry doctor to thank for a deeper understanding of the tradition of the *men's undershirt*. Another thing, he says poem 'po-*eem*.' He's follow-ing me around, trying to give me this and that secret message and stick his snake in me. I'm closed for business. His current oration:

frosh vitaman
the high man zoo
my nearest kin
the vilest stew

Where's Anna's new guy now? Marco the security drummer?

He's making out with Sarah in the bathroom now, they are in the shower in fact, meanwhile Ketchup is feeding Minuet a little shred of fruit roll-up in the kitchen. So whatever. Welcome to the dénoue-ment, that's all. I shouldn't get so horrified by the coupling because it's clearly a fluid thing and everyone's just doing what comes natu-ral, just sliding down the slide. Maybe I should try to seduce Minuet.

Anna is dancing and dancing, by herself, doing her unlikely muscle isolations, being strippery, the record resets and plays eternally. Her eyes? Spotlights. Her dress? Perfect. Sexy underwear was created with girls like you in mind. Your moon-white underwear is a beacon in the night, calling with the no-word language. I have to cover her butt cheeks entirely with my hands and squeeze them hard and she lets me, she goes kind of limp and sad. Okay okay I'm high. Okay okay I'll stop. I'll just watch. I would climb through one hundred earthen tunnels to get there, to be here with you. I would burrow under every lawn to arrive, to be with you. All your pretty shoes in a line. I would swim through every pool to get here. It cannot be explained in an equation. But now that I'm here and so close to her body, I'm an observer. I don't know how to act, to *do*. How long can this flamingo paradise heat last? How long does a woman wear sexy underwear before switching to more practical briefs? I could just say, *Let's make out*. I could just pull her hair. Pull her down. It's happened before. Oh, I don't care. She's just a stranger with shimmery alluring corn-white hair, she's just another person, we were just drunk, fuck it, boring, boring, boring, played, boring. But then, there is the place where the tips of her hair touch her neck and I am signed on again. And the needle drops and the record starts again. Some Girls.

BUGGY, DOONEY AND OTHER people I don't know arrive and some mushrooms are dropped under Buggy's tongue by the doetry pocktor.

How many did you put? Buggy asks with eyes ablaze. *Did you put a lot?*

Walls covered with curling worms and breathing camphor foam.

Softly heaving mesh, wall of fine fishes. Squares and cubes. Wall of soft foaming teeth now, ripple like worm-backs.

Me and Buggy roll into one thing, one tootsie roll, one rope of bread, one stick of clammy dough. My skin ends and his begins. In our interlocking rollick we crash into the tray of drugs and candy and spill it onto the carpet. As I roll over the Runts I feel them stud my back like goofy kisses. Little bananas. Part of a metric, fulfilling a zodiacal predestination, we roll up the walls and onto the ceiling, our skin salts conflating and our breath unnecessary. We are nutrition.

They fall like soldiers and the party ends, the party must always end, the record still spinning and resetting and spinning and forever. They look like soldiers too, as if dropped from a standing position, or even dropped from the sky—Marco snores on the floor under the bright chandelier, shielding his eyes. I turn the dimmer down, his lips smack as if to say *hey thanks*, and his eyes unsquint. Sarah and Ketchup are on the floor of their bedroom inside a fort, recoupled. Anna is on the couch with her face in the crack and Minuet curling against the inside of her knees. HER KNEES. Oh, inverted fruits of heaven! Alexis, the poor poetry doctor, is asleep on the porch clutching both his flask and also a near-empty bottle of Yukon Jack, and there is his twitching boot. Don't get a sunburn, Doctor. I consider writing HOMO on his forehead, but then I would have to hear the story every time I see him for the rest of my life. I switch the record player off now, a gray beetle of lint has collected on the stylus, I blow it away. Sleep has settled on the house like a lead blanket, frozen snow over tingling faces, but me, I don't even try to sleep. I do bunk down under the dining room table with a beach towel and a little pillow from the couch. A whiny ringing in my ears and the shadows still gritty, but

I'm approaching sobriety, I can feel it. I wonder if, as a baby, I never slept through the night. There is no one to ask! I will just have to wonder forever. Cheese n crackers.

When it's finally official morning I slip off, pull a red brassiere out of my hair, stumble into the world. A smashed piñata is bleeding blue dye into the street, watered by fine mist from the sprinklers. Its original form is indiscernible, something with limbs, a decorated dog or a horse with a saddle. A pink cake box open like a trout's mouth. A chaotic mandala of crumpled napkins and paper hats, a bag ripped open and gutted. A possum's wake? A band of rats? Cups with pink punch still rocking inside, bones, plastic forks with full mouthfuls still stuck on them. Oh, the riches. I poke the pink cake box with a long stick, opening it more. Who would throw out half a cake? I poke it lustfully, pushing the frosting off. I consider scooping up a handful and eating it, one soft mouthful after another, swallowing without chewing. Oh fuck yes. I could down a big chunk of that baby for breakfast. What people call breakfast. The sugar would burn.

A fat cockroach crawls at a mellow pace out of the bag and across the sidewalk, its antennas busy busy.

Hello, My brother. *Namaste*.

Spit Protect Us

I'M IN THE SAME surreal, itchy-verdant green meadow where Jorge and Beverly got married, that's where the officiate in her silly robes stood and held open a large black book like a photo album even though she only really needed one piece of paper. Suddenly I remember everything—the horrible dress I wore, the escape I made away from the party, Beverly in her purple boots and shiny nylons. . . . Time twitches and replays like a psychedelic record—the only real way to do something new ever is to leave, geographically leave. Right? Then you can really flip the record.

Kaia would not agree, Kaia would say that everything, everywhere, always, is made of the same essential material. I feel Kaia underneath my feet, supporting and meeting every footfall. When I was a kid, I pictured this essential 'stuff' that the universe is made of as something like dryer lint crossed with cloud. Speaking of clouds, they are turning pink, getting ready for sunset.

And up there is Old El Cid, still not speaking to me.

Señor Cid, I say. *Won't you talk to me? I and I? I need your consultation.*

He's not even looking at me.

El Cid, do you know Cid backwards is Dic? Can I call you El Dic? Because you're being a pretty major Dic.

I hold up my hands to feel some divine fornication or some surges of love or something coming off him but there is nothing. Maybe he's mad that I fucked someone else. Fuck you, then. I didn't even ENJOY it, okay???

My oracle's gone silent, so that's why I rustle into the prickly green like a rat. Through the green, and soon night is coming down and I move into the land of black and white, trees opening fists against the sky. Sleeping, snoring cobalt. Might have been wise to bring a flashlight. The terrain is steep here, then flat again and then steep, et cetera. I can see the backsides of the museums, all their grandeur sloughed away, the paint peeling off, their black garbage bags full of classy trash twinkling like giant raisins. It falls darker, the air cooler and wetter. Far away, the thorny dipping notes of a mariachi band, little stabs of sounds carried by the wind. Now it's dark-total, no city, no choppy sounds, no voices. I'm in a wilderness pocket, the grass tickling my eyes. I don't know my way anymore. Even the sound of the cars on the freeway is so faint that maybe I am imagining them. Maybe. Maybe I'll emerge from here, and maybe not. Maybe I'll emerge as something else, leaving my thin sheath of Nochita skin behind to be devoured by bugs.

As instructed, I turn left at the golf-club fence with the yellow plastic ribbon tied on it, walking toward the North Star. I can't possibly be doing this right, what am I, fucking Galileo? I am sure I am totally lost when the dog comes at me, he is murder lust from hell bounding towards my jugular.

It's nothing personal, he wants to kill everyone, Mother says, emerging from the blackness, shining a weak, amber flashlight. It is his righteous dogbeast nature. *He just loves blood*, she says, to put me at ease.

Just don't look him in the eyes. Just completely ignore him.

Mother sits on a cot in a cradle of leaves.

They kicked me out of the Pen, she says. *Too old, I guess.*

She wasn't kicked out, I know she wasn't, but I don't argue, that is her perception. Now she lives in the canyon near where the cops' horses sleep. Where pigeons come to die and ticket stubs come to weep. She lights a candle. I don't know if it's safe to light a candle here. I think it's probably not the best idea to light a candle here, there's a lot of dry brush and leaves. She insists on making me tea from wild plants. I accept but imagine all the plants around here are sticky with pesticides and runaway urine and illegally dumped chemicals. She shuffles for something in a big plastic bag.

She is trying to light a tiny stove, and the flame, when it takes, flashes the landscape into view like a cough of light. Plants and darkness cradle us. It's awful quiet.

Don't worry, I have knives, she says.

Don't worry, she says. *You can sleep here with me.*

I feel safe.

I don't feel safe, I just don't care.

OFTEN PEOPLE ASSUME *I'M a drug addict because I'm so deeply eccentric.*

She smokes at a joint, inhaling deeply in between proclamations.

You might think that, she says.

In fact I don't, I say.

You might think that. And so I want you to know that I do not do drugs. In fact I even have a phobia of needles. I could not be less interested. I'm weird enough sober.

She says that last line like she's said it many times.

When she goes off to pee I slip five fresh twenties into the breast pocket of her denim vest jacket.

Spit will protect us, she says.

She tells me how she was born rotten, with rotten blood, and how she wakes up every morning with a mouthful of blood. How she just wasn't made for these times.

In the distance, very occasionally I can hear what must be zoo animals trying out their wild night cries. I am so embarrassed for them. Mother sets up my cot. She snores softly throughout the night while I enforce closed eyes and move through layers of sound and sink through thick, staticky stripes.

I will open my eyes and be in Europe somewhere, wherever there are cobblestone streets with the stones set in circles, and labyrinths to walk, and pigeons with dignity. But no, I am in the bright-gray canyon, where I must immediately void such a shit. Maybe it was that psycho pesticide tea? I can't hold it, there's not even a question. I shit in a plastic bag and throw it down the hill. I wipe my ass with a found paper napkin, a clean one, thank you goddess.

In Europe, what would I do? What is Europe? Coffee? Castles? Tall shelves of books? Lean women? Sexual cigarettes.

Sexual Somnambulism

ALEXIS THE POETRY DOCTOR is having some kind of poetic freak-out, I don't know if he's joking or putting on a little show, he stomps down the steps in untied shoes, tosses the model volcano he's been building onto the lawn, it crashes violently and breaks apart, little pieces of foam rolling out. He's been doing speed, same old thing about adhering to some legacy and doing the best work he can do and defining for himself what is progress and what is poison. I sneak a look at his mannish, brown leather diary as he's ripping the volcano's core out of its pedestal and before each clump of text it is written:

Dear Good Biographer,

THEY ARE GETTING PALER, those sex-consuming party people. As they move deeper into coupleness. Anna and Marco, Ketchup and Sarah. They have a TV and they cuddle up and watch shows and eat vegan sushi.

He's not allowed to come, says Anna, nodding toward Marco, talking about her new place of employment, Nasty Nick's, the most popular strip joint on the strip, the sailor's choice. He is looking off. He has this problem where he picks his nose in public. Anna fingers the stringy banana-yellow garment which arrived in a padded brown envelope today through the mail slot. On this garment are sparkling puffs of golden thread, the size of cotton balls. She holds the things up to her chest, the puffies against her breasts.

I have really huge nipples, she says. *They're like freakin' sand dollars. These won't cover them.*

I think your nipples are right-on, I say. But actually maybe they are kind of ugly. In the light of day.

ON THE TABLE, ON top of the sweet vintage gingham tablecloth, is a collection of jumbo tubs of SmartBody vitamins.

Who's doing SmartBody? I ask.

I am!, says Anna. *They're the very best. They've cured cancer, and AIDS. It's been proven! Okay, well, they do actually make me eat less.*

I'm relieved to hear her say that because that's got to be the magic bullet that will cure me of my adoration for her, I mean if she becomes skinny and loses all her milky girlness, which is apparently what works best for stripping. Got to be, and I'm ready for that cure. I can't scrub my mind clean of the sight of her butt cheeks, two glowing mozzarella balls. I want to stick my nose between them and stay there forever, locked until my last breath.

Nasty Nick's

Oh god. Along the black walls are clinical diagrams representing different ways of fucking between man and woman, like a lifeguard manual. The one-armed save, the two-armed lift. The block, the shift, the wiggle. Buggy sits beside me, arms crossed over his jacket, mesmerized and uncomfortable. His eyes are huge and locked straight ahead, his jaw stiff and crunching. We sit in the dark area, where it feels like a theater.

Pour Some Sugar On Me kicks on and a woman comes out wearing a long, sheer red robe. Her thick legs swing and her splayed hands shoot out around her like fireworks, long red fingernails flashing as she swirls. She walks up and down the platform, performing her swiveling pelvis into the faces of various men. Some of the men she seems to know. She takes off the robe and there is her bare ass, big and fake-tanned and glittered, shaking and churning. It reminds me of a Christmas ham. It seems that she's having a good time. She looks about forty. I picture her on a jet ski, catching air on the bumps, her mouth open in joy, frosted hair whipping around her face, her hammy butt shaking. When the song is finished, she hurries to collect the money the men have put on the stage. A rehearsed congeniality pervades the exchange, an amicable trade remarkably free of subtext or shame or dark-side whatsoever. She puts her hand on one man's shoulder, says something into his ear, her tits knocking softly into his chin.

Allure is every woman's occupation if you think about it. Strippers and whores are just more real about it, Anna has said on more than one occasion. She admits that she goes back and forth about the spiritual healthiness of these lines of work, depending on whether or not she's working in them.

Buggy's eyes are spinning discs by the time that Anna emerges on the stage, a spider among hawks, a girl among women, wearing the spindly banana-yellow thing with the poofs and matching shiny yellow boots. Even with the tall boots, or maybe because of them, she is small, pixie, childlike. She wrangles out of the yellow thing and there are her tits, they seem immature, frozen buds. In this environment she does not succeed at being erotic. She stomps the ground with her great heels. The sound is loud, two wooden blocks slamming together, clomp clomp she goes, arms bursting out from her torso like a cheerleader, the yellow thing spinning around her wrist then flying offstage like a shot rubber band.

That was an off night, by the way. I think I felt that you guys were there and I couldn't do my character.

I don't want her to do her character. I do love that her stripper name is 'Kate.'

She ties a shred of a plastic garbage bag, torn up by Minuet, around my finger.

Now we're married, she says. *Kiss the bride*. She pulls my neck to her face and pushes her lips into my gums, her rubbery lips, forcing me to become her, forcing my face against her gritty map. I go. Bruised nipples, a skateboard broken in half, the ribbon of highway that stretches longer than a person can endure, gallons of vanilla extract, a lineage of bikinis, tongue against sand, collection of girdles sprayed with perfume to chase away the stink, the yearbook of men with wannabe Kinks haircuts.

I play with her yellow bikini outfit, hanging it over my ears.

Her head smells nice, it's a nice little head, it smells like apples, I like it against me. She likes to be played with, she's my girl tonight, she curls into me and falls asleep just like that, like a kitten. I want more but I just smell her and memorize the sounds of her, the feeling of her imprint.

No Hospitals

The Pen is especially dark today, someone put sheets over the windows and there are only the pink Christmas lights and a few religious candles in a cluster, mother Mary's hands embracing the warm red flicker, paraffin burn cheapening the air. I've come in from the bright sunny day and brought a pink box of donut holes. I don't see anyone but I sense a little scratching and stop and listen.

Help me.

Buggy naked, sitting in the corner, his hands behind him, the fish tank over his head, fogged moist by his breath. The bedding and carpet around him are dark with wetness and speckled with plastic seaweed and brightly colored pebbles like a sprinkle of stars. Naked naked boy man. There are his nickel nipples, a living heart beating behind them, a visible pulse even in the cool darkness. There are his two useless froggy legs and ugh, his little snout thing nestled in an obscene thatch of adult crotch hair. If I'm not mistaken, there is a small dead fish in one of the manfolds. I solve that problem by throwing a t-shirt over the region. He screams and recoils.

No! Fuck away! Don't want any cake wormy!

Buggy, it's Nochita. I'm going to take the fish tank off your head, OK?

He quivers in a way that I shall read as assent. I lift gently up. The glass case is heavy. He turns his head so I can get it over his funny nose. The wizened nose of a old man. He's shaking so bad. He'll be sad when he understands, he loved those fish.

Easy, easy. . . . I say.

Stop ripping out my hair!

His face is a fly's face, moist, his eyes thick and heavy and wobbling. His pupils are big and black, his mouth pressed tight.

You're alright, I say. *Don't freak out now.*

Role wormy. Cake wormy. Please you untie me?

His wrists are indeed tied together with a rope, I work on untying the knot, which has been pulled tight from resistance.

Stop fighting me, you're making it worse! I say.

Lemon pill. . . .

Buggy, did something bad happen? Or was this just fun?

Fun. Fun went too back bad. Bad baggy. Bag to bed.

I work open the loops at last and he thrashes his hands free and thrashes his whole body. He is breathing weird, sucking for breath now, bobbing with each hearty gasp. He puts his hands on my head and pulls himself to me, slurping and biting my neck. He smells like carpet, barn, ocean. His hair is wet and smells of mildew, an old wig found under the seats on a public bus at the end of the day, between a paper bag of spit-soaked sunflower seed shells and a can of beer. I fall into it. I say yes to it even though it makes me feel bad. He pulls my hair, keeps his head right next to my head, I can hear his rapid breathing into my ear, hot. He chews at my ear like a baby finding something for the first time. I hold him and pat his back, friendly friendly now. My fingers in his spine like locking into a gear. He holds on like a koala, sliding his feet around. He locks tight.

You shouldn't have killed the fish, he mumbles.

Buggy, I didn't kill your fish! Buggy, do you understand that I didn't kill your fish? I helped you, do you understand?

He stands up and there is his creepy baby small penis entity thing making another appearance, more substantial now, shapeshifter, unrolling. He does a shaky jig, then the crucifixion pose, freezes there, hands limp and swinging. I lift the fish tank onto a chair so he will not step on it at least. Gotta uphold the Pen policy: No Hospitals Never. Now he drops to his knees and holds on to my legs. Jeez. He pulls a blanket over his body and flips around like a child in tantrum, mumbling. Is this speaking in tongues? Something. He stops the thrashing and fingers the wall like a baby looking at himself in a mirror, talking sweet and drunk to his mirror-self. He pulls and pushes the blankets here and there, making arrangements. He picks up a plastic seaweed bush, draws it gently against his cheek, humming. He is a hundred people in one, doing different flashes of them all. Somewhere in the water-laden carpet are a few silver-shining fish corpses. Buggy pisses himself and the new moisture adds a fresh patch of shine to the wet. He's forgotten me and seems safe with himself so I leave, leaving the box of donut holes, they will make someone happy. Probably some cockroaches. Buggy is softly humping the ground. I want to put a dead fish in his asscrack to complete the tableau but I don't feel like touching a dead fish. Close the door softly. I think I did a good job.

Safe

Each breath takes its place after the one before it and before the one after it, lining up. Every breath counts until I'm dead. Lining up like an endless tin of sardines, a zigzag tire tread. Until I'm dead. I keep thinking of the Buggy's fish, they are tinned inside my head.

The leaves on the ground breathe like sleeping infants. So I kick them up. It's too bright, an aggressive, fresh Eden. Perfection, like the instant before the flower breaks its tiny neck and falls, before the bees fail and drop and die, before the sap drips into the black earth, making a coiled, concentrated perfume. The streets are endlessly wide, it's automobile Eden too. People sitting in their cars, driving. One person per car. Driving, driving, driving. Sitting there. Like human baseball cards. What if everything just froze like this. Everyone in their cars.

Walking on the great white bridge, I lean over the edge to watch the freeway. Populated peoples. Woman after woman wearing headphones jogs past me robotically, determined to have no exchange. When exactly do strangers break their routine and acknowledge each other? At what point are we willing to do that? For example, if I were climbing onto the ledge, about to suicide myself on down? Then of course a woman would stop and say:

> *No! Get down from there!* No she'd say:
> *Oh my God! Get down from there!*

But I am invisible. They look right through me and that seems right. A woman and a man approach, the woman holding a thin red leash connecting to an eager, small, blond-haired dog, the man pushing a baby carriage.

Are you alright, honey? she asks. Honey!

Oh I was just thinking about jumping, I say.

Their faces click into beacons of serious concern, his hand reaches out to me.

Oh, you're sweet. No, I'm not going to do it. I meant, I was thinking abstractly. Don't worry. Everything's fine. I'm sorry.

I really am sorry. Beneath us, on the scrappy green banks, rats lope in circles, in Celtic knots.

Do you see the rats down there? The rat families?

They don't answer, these poor decent people. They are looking at each other like, 'What to do in this situation?' I wonder if they are therapists. I wonder how often therapists marry therapists?

I PULL A GIANT mango, as massive as a football, down from a branch. I pick a tiny hole in it and begin the process of sucking the sweet juice and meat out. It will be a long process. It should sate for at least a day. What did I last eat? I chewed some ropey bread with the drugs. I am plush and content in my near-emptiness, every corporal faction blossoming against the wall of the next. This body is a miracle and the destruction of it is also awesome.

AT THE PEN AGAIN, the perpetual backstage, resting bodies are strewn about, as always I have to be careful where I step because there might be broken glass or someone's skull or elbow or ballsack or a dead fish or sexual intercourse.

Buggy sits like a Buddha in his corner. Towel over his shoulders, eyes closed, sitting up there like a child-king. And what a kingdom! Pulling one's own teeth, orgasming into a sock. His thin lips are mouthing a silent incantation or possibly twitching.

The man downstairs called the police, Buggy says, stepping on his smile.

The man made of wire? Why?

Because I pooped onto his patio, he says. He goes on toe-point.

The walls have been decorated with what looks like blood, big brown circles inside bigger circles, giant cells.

Nothing Ever Came of It

If the drugs are better in Canada, why not go to Canada?

And I've heard the cops don't have guns!

No guns? What do they have then?

Water guns.

Nerf balls.

Double-stick tape.

Everyone has the drug craving in common, but I don't really have it. I don't have much, and that's why this book will be short. Then nobody goes to Canada, the end.

Bitter

In a dream, a diaper system is connected to my baby's insides. Made by environmentalists, it only has to be changed every few days. It was difficult to install but worth it if you calculate.

I slept!!! I wake up in the urine gully, the niche next to the bathroom at Ancy Auto Repair.

Stupid gray light of dawn, this again, the traffic lights emerge, the daytime folks drive their sparkling cars, gigantified blind baby mice. Lady joggers again like automata corpses, their boobs again. Doctors, lawyers, makers of sound decisions. Those who crank the world to turn.

I trundle like a ghost through the town, my lips crinkled from dehydration. I drink from a hose.

Bobble-headed bitches. You're not pretty despite having made it your vocation. I will have to reschedule all of you. I hate all humans who are adults who exercise. But a little baby in a red dress in a stroller, she's right on.

You're getting bitter, you're young to be so bitter, Roberta had said, and the words roll around like a toy train in my brain. I don't really hate anyone. Check, please.

Gold Flecks

I'M TOO HIGH, I'M sweating, my heart is beating up my skull. Unsticking the cloth from my arms, my neck. It wasn't coke, it was speed! If I had known it was speed I wouldn't have done so much, every few minutes a new fresh jagged plastic burn experiment. I am inside-out and pop-eyed, my bowels flushed clean. I don't know the difference between coke and speed. Now I know. I march in place in the corner, steady of pace, letting the energy move through me, beholding my friends.

Who of you will survive, my transient kin? Some will die nobly, a car crash that wasn't her fault, a tumbling tour bus, others will die stupidly in public bathrooms at the mall, or stumbling off a cliff trying to find a place to vomit privately. Some will survive to remember these as a few funny, formative years. Alexis the poetry doctor, he'll be like that. He's wearing a paper bag on his head today, going apoplectic on a model volcano today, but in ten years he'll have tenure and kids, Jane and Jack. Anna will be one of those old ladies that wears lots of makeup and high-heeled sandals. A dry warm breeze against her crepey tanned neck. Buggy will stay stringy, become one of those installed local characters, a boardwalk fixture. Dooney will grow up, clear his throat, go to college. The man made of wire will keep sweeping forever, sweeping faster and faster, until he turns into a tornado and lifts into the sky, toe-tapping, leaving a white wisp between the clouds.

Okay, the walking in place thing didn't work. I keep going higher. My heart is a panicked butterfly. All my cells are bullets shooting in crazy coils like a jet-speed spirograph. Little eyelashes do their important little jobs, I blink, produce saliva, walk and somehow don't fall.

Last breath? Second to last? One of ten remaining?

I will keep walking. I will keep stopping and peeing and shitting if I have to. This is rock and roll. I will not twist and twist like a crocodile pulling stubborn flesh from a carcass in the water, I will not fight it. Let your heart shine out like a lantern. A nice place for a gaze to fall. Be a little baby who says Hi! in the night. Nobody would want me to babysit their child because I'm a certifiable degenerate. You can tell by the clenched hands. You can tell by the mean eyebrows. By the eyes that move this way that way. By the brow that is prematurely cleft from hard living. They don't know that I would treat the baby so sweet. I climb the wall, I climb the wall so fast. Suitcase in the hand, in the heart. A new home every day. When I grow up I will be a traveling saleswoman, a private contortionist, or a professional statuette. It's so cool when I bend over and my heart blossoms into my skull like a red sun.

Apparition

DESPITE THEIR POVERTY-AS-IT-IS-CONVENTIONALLY-KNOWN, despite the bare cupboards, the sour clothes and refried, jizzy socks, the feeding frenzy when I bring the pink boxes from the donut store, so desirous of food are they . . . they produce, from ears and assholes and blankets and pillowcases, pads of twenties when it's time to buy drugs. A fifty is conjured from under someone's eyelid even. The perfect amount of money is inevitably discovered. Yes it's true that I sometimes sneak my new-age money into pockets and backpacks but this materialization magic would happen anyway, it's independent of me. Some percentage of the body is always made of money.

Drugs again. The giddiness of acquisition, the ritual of sharing. Then we are all so so so smart. Buggy said that, that they make him feel so smart, and I find that to be the best description I've yet heard. For the speed anyway. Smart and fast and free from need. There is a little left, a little little little left, and then there is none left. That's a sad moment, when there's nothing left. It signals how we might have needs again. The night ends, a sigh, Buggy and Dooney fall asleep together like two baby kittens. Dumb scummy kittens. I rub the drug powder into my gums because everyone else is asleep and my gums are ringing like a bell. I don't care about the drugs, though. I get vicariously lustful but I never really want them, not like the others do. I am just a spy here. But I don't believe in wasting so I rub it into my mucosal membranes or whatever gums are.

Terminal Money

THE NEXT BOOK IS: *Hearth and Heart: In Kaia's Kitchen.* By Kaia with Roberta Freedom.

People just want to keep buying these stupid books.

The cover is a picture of the two of them in our old kitchen, each holding up a glass of bog slime, cheersing each other.

It's funny that you wrote a cookbook, I say. *Since Kaia never cooked?*

It has in it the foods she liked, Roberta snaps. *It promotes integral well-being.*

The kind of well-being that results in death at age forty-two? Preventable death?

Roberta looks at me like a social worker. Affectionate and appraising. Wants to know what I am eating and if I am drinking and how much. She gives me water and puts some drops of something in it, some special minerals. I've got to hand it to her, the water is delicious and feels great. I take a shower and accept some sea vegetable broth and close my eyes over the steam. And soon it will be time for the checkbook.

I'm not giving it to you anymore, Roberta says.

What!? Come on, be good!

You be good! You be fucking good! What are you doing? she says.

I'm good, I say. *I like my life. It's crazy sexy cool.*

She goes away and I know when she comes back she'll have the checkbook and I'm right, she does.

Here, she says. *This is your last check. Do you understand? I'm making a boundary here.*

I want to hear you say you understand, she says.

I understand, I say.

I know I've said it before, she says. *But this time I mean it.*

I fold the check and put it into my sock.

Kaia wouldn't have—

I don't hear the end of the thought because I choose to disappear. *Stay in touch.*

Tens

My fresh and final packet of money, all in tens which is my favorite money, makes my wallet fat in my pocket. If this really is my last storm of cash, what then? Makes me giggle.

I walk through the crusty sour patch of downtown to clear my mind. To pollute my mind. To take in the people.

Delicate and pale, with pink flesh and white hair, stooped, the old man ekes himself along bit by bit like a worm. There is something different about him, a disfigurement that I cannot place exactly. He turns to the side and I see what it is. It is that he has no nose. He has two black holes in his face instead, two hovering black bees, a Band-Aid covering them but not totally.

I try not to stare as we cross paths. I see his white wiry hair lifting from his neck in the breeze. The stains on his papery jacket. His expression is surprised, unchanging, his mouth an 'o.' In one hand is his cane, in the other a worn soft paper cup. He tilts the paper cup toward me. *Oh?* I see all this even though I am not looking, I am staring ahead. I lift my wallet from my pocket and put my money in the man's cup. All of my money. All of the money. His expression does not change, but he takes the money out of the cup and puts it slowly into a pocket inside his jacket and continues walking. Because he is no fool.

That's what happens if you snort too much drugs, says Dooney. *It does. You can get an infection in your nose and they have to cut it off.*

This guy didn't look like he did drugs, I say. *He looked like Santa Claus except he had no nose and he was skinny.*

Santa Claus does tons of drugs! Obviously!

Gas, Grass or Ass

Dean Jean, Mother P's *husband*, is out of prison now. Dean Jean is not a cowboy, he does not have a horse, but a workvan. He's muscular, large, and tan, like a professional wrestler. He calls Mother P his Little Lady and he does have a snakeskin belt, a bolo tie and a leather hat, like a cowboy hat except the brim doesn't curl up. A hand-rolled cigarette between his caramel teeth. I've agreed to drive with him to Oakland to help him *deliver a couch*, a euphemism that I don't investigate. I tell him I do not have a driver's license, only an expired permit, he doesn't care, he will drive. I can't tell if he's mad or if this is just how he is. After we drop off the couch I will go on to San Francisco, to deliver a suitcase of *Christmas ornaments* to a friend of Mother's called Maxxie Million. I have agreed to this, I've promised, Mother P has looked into my face and made me promise that I won't do anything weird or experimental, no experiments, this has to get to its destination, to Maxxie. This is kind of in exchange for the ride. Mother P is in the back of Dean Jean's van now in her sleeping bag with her usual *Was-I-just-hit-in-the-head-with-a-pan?* morning expression. Dean Jean lifts her gently up and out and puts her on the sidewalk, into a seated position. There is a real couch, I guess it wasn't a euphemism? We say a prayer that the couch will fit in the van and it does. Within minutes, Dean Jean and I are on the thick blank freeway, clocking miles underneath us like nothing, nothing at all, like a spaceship, like pages flipping. I can't believe how fast you can change your life.

Everyone in every other car has a name and their name is *IDIOT!* or *FUCKING moron!* The needle bobs around *Empty*, I wonder if we will run out of gas and roll like a marble onto the shoulder and then what? Start a new life between two dry bushes? Rub some sticks together? Roll-your-own tampon.

Don't worry. That gas thing hasn't worked since the day I bought it. I do it by mental calculation.

What a relief!

WHAT DO YOU DO with your very last dollar?

Well I find mine in my pocket. I buy a coffee at Peppy's Trucker World, and as I'm paying I realize I probably should have purchased something like maybe a candy bar with nuts, something with protein. I put lots of milk in the coffee, there's your protein. It's possible that Dean Jean could drive away without me and I am warm to this possibility. He is unpredictable and has many threads of things always happening in his scabby mind. He's out there waiting for me though, scratching hard at a spot on his scalp. Maybe he's doing a gas calculation on his scabby scalp abacus. By the way, he'd like to clarify, he never told Mother P that thing, about that the dog was going to eat her. She was making it up. And he never hit her. He loves Mother P, he loves his wife, but come on, she's a little crazy. Anyone with two eyes can see that. Even with one eye. He loves her though. He missed her so bad when he was locked up. That's how he knew he wanted to marry her, because he didn't forget her. He never forgot her face, it stayed precise. He feels her waiting for him now, two cots in the canyon, Spit watching over her. She's delicate, she needs a protector. He knows what she needs.

You don't think the cops will pick her up?

They better not, he says.

THE FREEWAY IS NOW a smooth straight vein. I like when he's not talking. I like it when he's not smoking. He is continuously doing both. His chapped lips are amazing.

The calculation is correct. It is correct. There's no doubt in my mind, he says. Tap tapping the dashboard.

I can see his teeth through his cheeks. His eyes are buzzing like beehives. He never eats.

It's gonna be a nightmare man, like something from the bible. No effing doubt in my mind. Do you know what it will be like? I do. That's why I take a wind-up radio with me everywhere. Everywhere I fucking go. We're going to break off, snap, like a little, a little piece of stale bread. Half of this state's gonna float off into the Pacific. No one can deal with it, no one can deal with the truth, but I can't help but see it, I see it so clearly in my head. I see the women crying and the kids fighting with dogs over the last Oreo. I see everyone sick with diarrhea and people gnawing on leaves just to wet their dry mouths. You think it's science fiction, right? You'll see. Off the radar, off the fucking, what do you call it, geiger counter.

Richter scale?

That's it, smartass. The fuckin Richter scale's gonna be snapped in half like, like a piece of stale bread crust. Snapped right at the seam. It's gonna be awful, man.

He seems delighted.

Maybe it'll be fun, I venture. *Maybe we'll start a new world.*

You're an idealist, pal. I'm a realist. It's going to be hell, and no one's going to believe it, cuz no one saw it coming. But I did. I saw it coming. I'm saying it plain, for the record.

For the record, at the next gas station is a young woman with skim-milk-colored skin and three blue dots tattooed under each eye, fat black dreadlocks and a big black shining dog, she's going to Oakland too. Sure there is room, she can ride with us. She and the dog crawl into the back, arranging themselves onto the couch. The way we had to cram the couch back there, its hind is elevated, so if the van doors came open somehow, this girl would slide right out onto the I-5.

I'm vegan, but my dog isn't, she says. For the record.

I can sleep anywhere, she says. *I slept right in the middle of the highway once, right on the yellow line.*

I think we eat really well actually, she says. *You wouldn't believe what people throw away. I think I eat really healthy. I don't pay for food.*

She falls asleep back there.

Three

Welcome

A WAXY MANNEQUIN GAZES serenely toward the moon in the frame of a yellow window above us. A bicyclist wobbles by as the girl and her dog scoot out of the back of the van, she's rubbing her eyes. This is her destination, the crookedest white Victorian on the block, a decrepit, charming wedding cake of a house, with white rubber snakes hanging down from the porch ceiling.

Dean Jean is tired. The girl says we can stay here, if we want. Everyone here is peaceful and kind and we are welcome.

As usual I like being underneath the table. If there was a blanket that does not smell like throw-up or piss or wet dog I would like it. Thank you but I do not really need a blanket. I am oddly warm. If I had a baby I could cuddle with it right now and that would be nice.

Dean Jean and the girl go into one of the rooms and click the door closed very softly, and that's when I realize that he's going to fuck her, duh. I am so slow and infantile about these adult things. It's like I am missing some essential programming. I wonder if I will tell Mother P, if I *should*. If *a woman should tell a woman*. Woman. Mother P, chin-deep into her sleeping bag, alone in the canyon, the critters hooting and zeroing in, her eyes moving back and forth tick tock tock, Spit asleep at the foot of the cot, while Dean Jean looses this teenager's titties from her sticky bra. Away, away, away.

The Bridge

I SLEPT LAST NIGHT. I slept like babies and dogs and dolls do. I stayed there until I'd had enough, then rose with a full tank of energy, a cool and clear mind, cheeks pink and warm. It happened to *me*. The air was ripe and cool when I stepped onto the porch to see what "Oakland" was like in the sun. Oakland had a reputation for being a place with some soul. I beheld a row of immense, haunted Victorians in easter egg colors, leaning a little this way and that way, like a tipsy choir, and the white clouds above like hot bread cracked open and pulled apart, waiting to be devoured.

DEAN JEAN INSISTS ON driving me to San Francisco from Oakland, even though there is a train that goes right from here to there, he's trying to win my favor so I don't tell Mother P about his wandering snakeskin dick, I guess. Then we're supposed to go back to San Diego. The skim-milk girl gives us a grocery bag of nuts and dumpster-dived bread for our journey.

Across the epic elastic orthodontia of the bridge and toward the foggy dip of city we sail, I sense a heavy looming enchantment. Mirrors, bells, banners, marimbas, pleasant alarms in the heart, I am secretly invisibly welcomed. We'll see. We roll in. A spindly gamb crowns the highest hill, forms a kiss with her metal mouth and winks. Army of orange and pink domestic lights on the slopes are greeting torches, invitations to the colorful carnival. It's a special hour, the sky a sacred blue, cobalt glass mixed with water, blue as a bell. The stars are just arriving, growing, the fully developed ones like holes poked through paper, one great yawning cathedral. A bird's trembling flute song. Not native, but who is native? A man with a bird on his shoulder, his very best friend. Mystery bookshop. Families made from matchsticks, solid as trees. Millions of stories fossilized into rock. Distillate, the full spectrum of feeling, of color. The ecstasy of my tongue in my mouth. Inanimate things seem to be smiling. A garage door with a mural of a man's hairy asscrack, a vehicle in the shape of a cat's head meows by, a woman spraypaints a wig silver on the sidewalk. I don't want to be unreasonable but this place seems to have a spirit and it seems to connect with me like a buckle. The traffic is bad now, because a naked cyclist is getting arrested, glittering drool, attracting a small crowd of gleeful onlookers. On one building, couches are crawling out of windows. I am feeling a little drunk on it all, I am wanting to melt out the window and pool into a puddle and be part of it. . . .

Dean Jean is increasingly agitated and shiny and in need of drugs so I've become mostly invisible. I feel like a box full of things. When he parks the van to cop, or find a bathroom to tap and drain out his poisonous liquids, I make sure he's out of sight then make my Hollywood gunslinger escape. Hesitating for a moment, deciding whether to grab the 'Christmas Ornaments' or leave them and be totally enencumbered. A vision of Mother P's terrified face prompts me to grab the suitcase before kneeing the van door quietly closed, walking in the opposite direction from the one he took, looking cool real cool, that's the secret is just look cool, I am just clutching this rather heavy fraying suitcase. But I am so overcome with delight alloyed with a bit of terror that when I hit the next block I must run, I am off like a slingshot, I run block after block until I exhaust myself completely and collapse beneath a small fresh tree behind a hot yellow gas station. I melt into a volcano of laughter, it is too good, the tree was waving at me, the tree took me, Dean Jean will never find me, no one will ever find me and I am free, safe, I will just keep this suitcase in between my knees. I feel like I've just gotten married, to this place, whatever this is.

But you know how marriage goes. The bloom fades and so on. Not really, I am still in love I just I get hungry. I have no money and I need to get rid of this stuff. In my ecstatic fugue state, well, let's just say I don't have that piece of paper with Maxxie's address and I don't remember it by heart. I am seeing the number 666 in my mind, but that is just my mind playing a trick on me probably, how clever. The temperature drops fast when the sun goes down, and being cold sucks. This is the 'weather' people talk about. I get it now. I don't want to go to jail and I need to fulfill my promise. I walk a little more, then find a car wash to repose myself against and I dream that I am eating the corner of a concrete building. Dean Jean rounds a corner and I don't fight him, he slits me open from ear to belt with a small, efficient blade. But it was only a dream.

In reality, a lady steps out of a clean gold car, her calves pouring perfectly into her priceless red pumps (evolution!), gives me a delicious sandwich wrapped in white paper and a bottle of coke. And a fifty-dollar bill.

Mercy

IS THIS THE CITY I've been hearing about?! The city where animals come for mercy?

Two hookers fighting over a dead pigeon, both teetering, enormous, pushed-out Neanderthal foreheads, both with spiny lobster hands. The blonde wears Band-Aid-colored make-up but it fails to spackle shut her deep constellations of blemishes and sores, the spectacle made more grotesque by the attempt at subterfuge. I move out of the way, pigeon feathers flying, I clamp shut my sinuses like barn doors. It's just a case of not sleeping, don't mistake it for truth . . . don't forget. . . .

It's night, the streets shift and slither with life. Colored lights, clunky dancing neon women crudely stabbing at allurean invitation, up to no good. Raggedy dolls stitched poorly together, damp stuffing bursting out from the seams, pencil shavings and bacon bits. A dress made from a chain link fence. A man is lying down in the street, the middle of the middle lane, in the crucifixion pose, a fallen Mayan god. He blends exactly into the black asphalt, total camouflage because he's wearing a large black hat and black shirt. If you were a car coming downhill it would be very hard to see this figure and if you wanted to change lanes you would very easily run right over him. Like this car that is coming down upon him, it slows and honks, drives around him like a confused ant. I go to him, stand above him as a human flare. I don't want him to be run over, at least not right in front of me. I intercept his invitation to death.

Hey, wake up, I say down to him. *Are you dead?*

Mother P told me once about how you could tell if someone is asleep or unconscious by rubbing the center of the chest, hard, with your knuckles. I rub him with there with the tip of my shoe and he doesn't rouse. But he's not dead because he's breathing a little, I see now. His face is smooth and dark, relaxed, peaceful. He looks like a healthy man, his apple-shaped middle rising and falling. His hat is a rich black and very big, it looks expensive.

I just keep on standing there. I move a little when the cars come so that they will see me. Our eyes are better at seeing things in motion, Dean Jean told me all about it, how we are designed for that, we are apes. Speaking of apes. . . .

The cops arrive, with sparkling lights but no sirens, they hop out of the car like quick clowns, snap on purple latex gloves in unison and drag the man lovelessly to the sidewalk by his armpits. The hat topples off his head and rolls underneath a parked truck, no one makes a move to retrieve it. They drop him gently, lean him against a building.

Wake up amigo! yells a woman cop, tapping his thick leg with her boot, shiny and black like an olive. I find the hat under the car and toss it onto the man's lap.

STUNNED SOLDIERS YANKED FROM the trenches, seized from the ectoplasm, blinking and doubting, confused, trying to crawl. Zombies, flesh unraveling in strips, meatball-faced, dragging themselves down pocked gritty alleyways, covering their sensitive newborn eyes. In sour fetid lots they sit completely still like meditators, needles hanging from abscesses, syringes bobbing in the breeze. Needles are here and there, taxis run over them, high heels step on them, sensible shoes avoid them. Open mouths, parchment skin, a hospital bracelet gracing each wrist. A flying skeleton swooshes past me, her clothing stretched tightly over each rib, her eyelids painted red. Her breasts are coconuts shoved violently under her skin.

I have to keep my eyes moving, if they settle on one thing for too long the image will get burned in.

Samples of piss and blood in jars, a baby's lost shoe, a flyer on a telephone pole seeks a teenage girl. Another note on another telephone pole beseeches, *Chui Zang! You missed your court date. Call collect immediately*. Call, Chui. Not fade away Chui. A man sits on a bus bench, a great lump above his eye, swollen nearly shut. A woman holds her child's hand, the child's octopus legs swimming in blue sweatpants. They disappear into the bus. A claw reaches out to nab me from a window but I swat it away, it leaves a dark film and a campfire smell. I look for a place to run, but then I see the number on the building and realize I am here, at my appointment. Am I really? This can't be the place. I push the button and I am buzzed in.

First I need to wash my hands, I say, when he opens the door.

I know—gross neighborhood right? But we got such a cool space! Look at this pinball machine. It's vintage, the real thing.

His black jeans are brand-new, stiff and inky. He wears two pagers, one on either side. Surrounding him is a gaggle of young women stuffing their hair into wig caps, arranging breasts into bras, buckling shiny shoes, counting money, cigarette cartons, and smoking.

How old are you? he says, chewing his pen.

Twenty-one!

Good answer, ha ha ha.

Even though he usually hires only friends, he will give me a whirl. Business is booming and he will give me the chance, because he can tell I'm smart. He can tell I will be one hundred and ten percent reliable, which is what's required here.

666

I HAVE A FEELING about it, this stylistic anomaly of a building that looks like a dash of Florida budget-retirement in the midst of downtown San Francisco. Something tells me.

But the woman at the front desk tells me that there is no one there called Maxxie, Max, Maxine, Maxwell, Million, Thousand or anything like that. I don't have any more information or ideas so I sit at a bench outside of a laundromat across from 666 Ellis and watch people come and go, looking for someone who might be Maxxie, thinking of what I will do with this stuff if I never find Maxxie. This suitcase is in a way my best friend, and in a way my Achilles heel. I am thinking deep thoughts along these lines when a man comes out of the laundromat and tells me to leave right now, because I am not a customer.

A SMALL MAN EMERGES slowly from 666, his head covered in a bubblegum-pink scarf. It's that blot of color that gets my eye. I can't tell his age, if he is either old or just tired? Is he beautiful? He's not. So it can't be my guy. Right? Still I follow him down the street.

Maxxie?

Yes honey, he says, not looking back at me. *I'm just leaving to see the doctor.*

Mother P sent me! I say. *You know Mother P? From San Diego?*

He stops walking and turns to me now, condenses his eyebrows, eyes the suitcase. The scarf on his head is actually a towel, a small pink towel with orange roses all over it. He eyes me from top to bottom and back to the top like an elevator, his eyes turn on and his grim mouth ripens and smiles.

Oh, yes! You're the doctor, then! Thank you doctor!

He kisses me on my cheek and he smells like a sweet old church.

Mother had described Maxxie as glamorous, dangerous, devastatingly beautiful 'in a kind of Spanish way,' and often dressed as a female flamenco dancer. She'd said he might be found doing some kind of performance with a Victrola, you know, the old kind of record player thing that you wind up? I hope this is the right guy. This Maxxie before me wears a red velour sweatshirt with LADY embroidered on it in shiny black thread and a brown stain in the middle, shiny black pants, and dirty white sneakers with fat laces untied. He has a spray of tiny dark moles all over his neck, stars in reverse. And then that towel on the head. I'm just not sure.

You know Mother, right?

Of course, he says. *How's her . . .*

He makes a swirling motion with his finger around his head.

. . . her hair? he finishes.

Got my man.

HE INSISTS I COME up to his room, stay a minute. If anyone at the front desk asks who I am, he's going to say I'm his physical therapist. So look official, look healthy, look like you've been here before. But better if I walk exactly to his right, real close next to him, so they don't notice me at all. There's a strict visitors policy. Just be cool it will be fine. We make it past, into the cattle elevator, down the plaster hallway with dim buzzing lights to number 6. He unlocks the door and enters his apartment carrying the suitcase on one hand like a cocktail tray.

Look what the doctor brought us, girls!

It's not really an apartment, I mean it's a room, packed tight. There's a small television—the picture's on, but no sound—with a woman horizontally under it, and one on a cot beneath the ironing board too. A fuchsia dress sealed in a plastic bag hangs from the light in the middle of the room. There is a third woman emerging from the stove, uncurling vertically.

Lots of bodies saves on heat!, Maxxie says, gesturing to everything.

A large dog waggles out from the bathroom and walks right into me, crashing his nose into my crotch.

Look, she peed, that means she likes you! Fluffer, stop peeing, I don't have any more paper towels!

I learn that discussion or mention of the size of the dog versus the tiny apartment is forbidden. I learn that the others rarely leave the room, because they're not supposed to be living here and the more they come and go the more likely they are to be caught. And anyway everything they need is right here. Each one gets their own shoebox for toiletries and medications.

They vet me in a sisterly way. Someone finds a zit under my bra strap and squeezes it, a good one she says, a real snake-in-a-can. Another pushes me in the small of my back. One wants to know if I'm a dyke.

Let's not be mean, Maxxie says. *She's a friend of Mother P's, let's be kind to her.*

Okay, are, you, a, dyke? She asks slower and in a higher pitch. I don't know the right answer and the question tickles. I open my hands like *I don't know*.

What is this building? Is it a hotel? I say.

It's a special place for special people.

You have to be insane and indigent, says a lady from the kitchen counter where she reclines, nuzzling a carrot.

And very glamorous, says Maxxie. *Mostly glamorous.*

We're taking Fluffer for a walk. Maxxie is wearing slippers and he shuffles, it's annoying me, also his buttcrack shows.

Look that's my car, he says, and points to a glistening new silver Mercedes, parked on the street. *Want a ride?*

Okay!, I say, playing along. The hubcaps glitter like diamonds. He's getting very close to the car and there is a red light blinking in it and I am afraid he will set off the alarm or that the owner will emerge and smash him in the head. Maxxie touches the door handle and an alarm goes off, a shrill deafening clamor.

Fuck, he says, presses something on his keychain, the alarm stops.

I have to move it anyway for street cleaning, he says. *So get on in!*

I've never been in a car like this. The door goes *tick* when it closes, and my body slips in, sliding against the seamless black leather. The smell of the leather is intoxicating, pervasive, soothes me like a drug, and I fall asleep and wake up at the beach. Fluffer and Maxxie are playing on the shore, Maxxie is wearing a large white sunhat, he tosses a stick and Fluffer bounds after it.

Back near 666, we drive around for a few years looking for a free parking place. I still don't understand where the car came from or who it really belongs to and I've given up trying to figure it out. I accept all things as impermanent.

We find a place to park finally. There's a person sleeping on the curb, one of her pigtails dangling down into the gutter, Maxxie pulls the car in very carefully so as not to hit her head.

Don't you ever get freaked out? Of all the zombies in this hood?

I don't scare easily, he says. He unwraps a granola bar for Fluffer, her favorite.

Blonde

IT'S A BLONDE BOB that falls to my shoulders. Maxxie brought me here because Charlie's Fancie Wigs is the very best in the world. Charlie works on me with small expert hands, he tugs and pushes and flattens, sets the hidden straps around the bones at the back of my skull. He trims the bangs to hit just below my eyebrows and layers them so they fall in natural looking pieces.

Like a James Bond girl! I love it!, Charlie says.

You're so blonde!, says Maxxie. *You look good blonde!*

It's a go.

Thank you, I say to Maxxie, kissing him on the cheek as we jaunt down the street, me holding my new secret identity in a plastic bag.

At 666 I put it on again to show the girls.

Now your lips, says Fendi, opening her toolbox full of makeup. She sands my lips down with something, daubs a glob of gloss on them. Maxxie does my eyes, sheathing my lids in charcoal and violet.

When I'm declared complete and I behold myself, I am a stranger. A sexy, dangerous, total stranger.

Helloo, lady. Some gloss gets on my teeth, I wipe it off with my finger. I must be careful not to let strands of wig hair touch my lips because they stick forever and mess it up.

Souffrir pour être belle, says Fendi, from her row on the bookshelf. *You'll get used to it. You are moving stiffly, but you must appear fluid, like a lily in the breeeeze. . . .*

Maxxie'd learned to do makeup in prison. A fellow prisoner, Lala, made her own makeup by scraping magazine pages with her one special long fingernail until the pigment came off in a powder, then she emulsified it in her spit and painted her face, and she always looked dazzling. She also stuffed the back of her shoes with paper so that she had some "lift." Not only was she gorgeous but she had a heart of gold and she never lost her dignity, never, no matter what. I imagine the guards going stiff and silent as she glided by.

Car Predators

BOUNCING ON MY THICK soles down a wet silver street. Car predators swinging all around, sniffing out slow pedestrians to scatter and squash. Indeed a few go down, it's not pretty. Poor lady's purse splits open like a dropped watermelon. Lipstick and a roll of quarters and a bunch of other things roll out, a firecracker of little things.

Oh, oh, she says, touching her head then looking for blood on her fingers. *Oh boy*.

She crawls up. The car has run away. She's brushing the filth off her pantyhose. She finds her wallet under a parked car's tire. She limps on. She's okay.

People pop back up from death around here like cartoons. Life is elastic. You get more than nine tries, plenty more. Who knows how many more. You can just get back in line and get more and more lives.

Bouncing on my thick soles down a wet silver street. Car predators flying around on bat wings want to slay me, split me, spill me like a bowling pin, send me dripping into the rain drains. I have to leap away from them, press myself against walls to avoid their rocket-fast blows. I'm getting good at it. The sun is slipping. It goes dark and I am patting the cool buildings and bicycles and grinning specters of parking meters to find my way.

Je M'appelle

Golden epaulets dangle from my shoulder shelves, bands of golden twisted twine pulled taut across my chest.

This number's just a little small on me, I say, pulling down the skirt, trying to arrange it to cover a majority of my ass.

No no, that's perfect. You just have to get some little shorts to wear underneath, says the man in the black jeans.

One of my rows of fake eyelashes falls off and a nice girl helps me reapply, blowing to make the glue tacky before pressing it back onto my lid.

Don't itch them, she says.

I walk along Columbus Street with spidery ancient legs of creaking maritime wood, the pillbox hat pinned into my wig's fake scalp. In and out of the bars.

I'm a cigarette girl, and the tray I carry on my body is a buffet of basic carnival pleasures. Cigarettes of course, but also lighters, cigars, light-up fake roses, parlor tricks, candy-colored condoms, those stupid pens where you turn it one way and the girl's shirt peels off. The waters part for me naturally, as if I were doing something important or noble. Packs of boys in white baseball hats break up so that I can pass through, couples unchain. I hypnotize. I don't even have to say the silly refrain, *cigars, cigarettes,* as others say this as soon as they see me. For the first hour or so no one buys anything, but then the bills begin to fall into my hands like sleet. I guess people get drunker and need cigarettes, or are more lonely and want to talk to me. I'm there. There for you. I suck moist money from pockets, a magnetic force. Dollar bills turn over into twenty-dollar bills. A woman loves me. A woman hates me, doesn't want her boyfriend talking to me, she positions herself to block his vision.

We don't want anything, she says.

But look, it's a rose that lights up, I say.

The man buys the light-up rose for her and she is delighted, she puts it in her cleavage.

A drunk man with long hair gives me a twenty for no reason, slaps my palm.

I don't know why I just did that, he says.

Take it back, I say.

No, no, he says. *It's yours, keep it.*

In this way money becomes very elastic. Maxxie was right, he had said I would be good at it.

Halloween

I'M A DIAMOND DOOOOG, Maxxie says into to the air as we bobble off the bus, him clutching the rail, teetering on the pink stilettos he calls his 'muffins,' why 'muffins' I don't know, an empty plastic bag taped to each heel. He doesn't walk well in heels. His scant black hair is swung up at the crown like a baby's, and his face is painted clean, his eyesockets silver flowers, his mouth redrawn in red. I too cannot walk in heels, and the black glittering boots are wasted on me, they are heavy and as useless as hammers as I try to make my way off the bus and into the party with a crumb of charm intact.

It was Maxxie's idea to dress me as the murdered Nancy Spungen, he got inspired, he sacrificed my wig, colored it with markers and curled it, and burned it with a curling iron. I'd needed a new one anyway, he said, since I didn't TAKE CARE OF IT. He'd ripped up something and made it into a miniskirt with safety pins. Fendi gave me expert track marks and convincing bruises on my legs, arms, and neck, and insisted that I wear these boots.

Honey, you have something stuck to your shoe, says a man from a bicycle.

I know!, shouts Maxxie.

Everyone, everyone, is compelled to tell him about something being stuck to his shoe. Meanwhile I can smell the makeup melting on my face. Recipe for making friends: a plastic bag taped to your shoe plus public transit plus San Francisco plus Halloween.

Tonight everyone has rolled out of their niches, sniffing for trouble. A wild parade fills the blocked-off streets that seethe with every imaginable flavor of vice, chainsaw shows, magical candy necklaces. Things disappear into mouths. There's a lot of naked butt cheeks and a pair of chubby girls with matching horse bridles. Maxxie knows everyone everywhere, and does not refuse any offered substance. Everyone talks very loud. Suddenly I want only to nestle into a warm soft bed. I have little interest in pressing my tits into the glass wall of a fancy restaurant as Maxxie insists that I do, or drinking the spit of strangers. I want to piss in toilets only. I want to wash this makeup off my face.

Are you feeling boring, honey? Fendi asks. *It's the pills. They do that sometimes.*

I want to go to bed, I say. I didn't take any pills. Wait, yes I did. Fendi gave me something, I forgot. Klonnie. It seemed like just a little nothing. I want a bed, a room with a little lamp. A little glow.

What you need honey, is some coke.

I don't want coke, or anything to wake me up. I want to sleep. I don't want to *not want to sleep*. I want to sleep. I have crashed through this threshold. It feels like a coming-of-age. Tonight is my quinceañera.

Maxxie *really* wants me to smash my tits into a restaurant window. To amuse him and to startle the yuppies. *It's politicallll*, he whines, spanking my butt softly. *They think they can just buy their way in*, he says. Finally, I do it. I do it pretty good, pulling my shirt up to my chin and and winding my body into the glass to Maxxie's squeals of delight until everyone in the restaurant has looked up from their butter-rubbed roast chickens or wood-fired pizzas or truffled french fries and tinkling drinks and the whole restaurant seems to be silent and agape, it feels pretty good and the maître d' is storming outside to shoo us away but we slip into the mass before his rage can land on us, moving as quickly as I can in these fucking shoes, I put away my tits

. . . Maxxie is delighted for a long time, telling everyone what I did and mimicking for them my little dance and exaggerating every time.

SOMEONE GOT SHOT SO the street party got shut down, so we head to the Motherload.

Halloween night is like any meat-packed night at the Motherload except crazier, more fake blood and fake bad teeth mixed in with the genuine bad teeth. The surfaces are covered in driblets of white wax, decades of it, so it's a dirty icicle cave or a mountain of solidified semen, the eighth wonder of the world. Maxxie demands a straw with his vodka tonic then sucks the whole thing down in one suck then asks the bedraggled bartender *is that the best you can do for me, papi?* The bartender in his white undershirt and fake slashed face hates Maxxie immediately, but Maxxie will not unclench the limelight with his rectum, he thinks he is holding court. He is told to not dance on the pool table. He ignores this directive. Someone rips one of the plastic bags from his heel and he gets mad.I get him down, I pull him down, he is strong, he crawls right back up, slow and unsmiling. Like a helium balloon he rises over and over in his teetering 'muffins' to dance on the pool table. To shake his tubby rump on the pool table. To wave the plastic bag around. Nobody likes him and they don't like me either, because I am with him, because I am a woman, because I am covered in tracks that look real? Finally I stop trying to get him down, I give up. The bartender and the hunky bouncer come up and say *okay, okay, time to go, guy* they remove Maxxie swiftly from the pool table and pull him by both his meaty biceps towards the door as he thrashes and goads, *ay, papi!*

I have been *kicked out* of the Motherload! I can't wait to tell

Maxxie when he's in his right mind! Oh Maxxie. Oh single plastic bag hanging on.

The black chill is sudden and sobering, my eyes are raw from the makeup. I want to get us in a cab, but there are no cabs. There is never a cab. The cabs have all disappeared from the earth. So we walk slowly down Folsom Street. I keep my arm around Maxxie as he scratches along, I keep him moving in a straightish line.

He slips from me and drops suddenly to the sidewalk, landing on his skull with a *tonk*. No hands moved out to protect him, it was like a dropped baby. He is face down now, not moving, and I am thinking he is dead and my heart starts to thump, but when I roll him over his skull is all intact and he is breathing, even smiling, his eyes look alive rolling around up there and he emits a little growl. That was close. I should have been holding him tighter. I help him up by the armpits. No blood anywhere. No bloody surprises. The last thing that happened in his life will not be getting kicked out of the Motherload. His last words will not have been *But I loooooove Queen, let me dance it's not a crime you fucking nazis!!!* as they swung him matter-of-factly through the saloon doors into the piss-perfumed alley.

A few paces later he touches his eyebrows. An egg is growing.

Did I fall? My head hurts.

I help Maxxie pull his pants back up after he pisses in the bushes in front of his apartment building. I keep hold of his shirt, I stay right on top of him this time, not wanting him to fall again. I stay close to him even in the elevator, I hold him tight.

Backstage

I WISH I HAD a camera because Maxxie's stone-still face, his chin on the coffee table, the makeup disintegrated into a gray swamp of its noble intention, his beauty having crumbled, his eyes falling down his cheeks, the now-solid brown lump protruding proudly from his forehead, is worth documentation.

IN THE CURVING SILVER valley of an abalone shell is a tiny brownish-gray booger, a meaty grain of sand, maybe one quarter the size of a popcorn kernel. Maxxie tilts it up so I can see.

That teeny thing?

That's it, Maxxie says. *That's my kidney stone.*

He pats his belly.

They're not supposed to give it to you, he says. *But the nurse liked me. You can touch it.*

ONE TIME, WHEN HE was a junkie, he was too high, he was just watching the curtains breathe, they were perfect, and it was the most blissful moment in his life. A friend found him, put him in a cold shower and probably saved his life. She was shrieking in Maxxie's ear and Maxxie was thinking no, no, I'm so happy, leave me alone, I'm drifting toward the light, to the gates of heaven, everything is finally good. The friend squirted cold water in his ears and that's why he survived. It was the water in his ears, he's sure.

And, the closest thing to giving birth was passing a turd when he was a junkie. From this he empathizes more deeply with the woman in childbirth. This is why he understands women so much.

Anointing

I'VE ESCAPED TO THE main library again. I am going to hit the career section, I swear, but first I am just going to check out some CDs.

It's a sound with hard wet edges. I'm examining The Best Of Turkish Pop when the object hits me, right where the neck meets the shoulder, the center of my tender curve. It's not an acorn, shoe, or book, it's the fibrous spawn of an old man's throat, spit from stories above. It was cool by the time it reached me, and hard, I thought it was a book at first, its impact was that strong, but then when I touched it I realized it was bio. A security guard extends a gloved hand. What would this city do without latex gloves? I'm kind of whimpering. I feel panicked. He stays cool, takes me to the secret security clubhouse, wipes me with a paper towel while humming a song. He wipes my fingers and between my fingers and my neck with a rough paper towel as I rock. Then he sponges me down with some foamy antiseptic. His touch is sweet, actually, almost motherly. I kind of relax into it. Soon I feel cleaner than before.

A wall of polaroids is the saddest collection at the library. Some stare into the camera as if it were the camera that had brought the harm unto them. Others do not show their feelings, curling into themselves or hiding behind hair, some are blurry, unwilling to comply and be still, a black mouth smeared open or baring teeth. Most were caught vandalizing or stealing books, my sweet nurse explains. So they're not allowed in the library anymore. I feel a torrent of compassion for them tear open in my heart. Have sadder words ever been spoken than 'not allowed in the library anymore'? Here are kids who fell off their bikes and never got back up. Her, her teeth will never grow back in. He never learned his colors. He, wrongly imprisoned for seven years. They will take the man's picture, the one wizard who spat on me. He is actively psychotic, responding to things in the air all around him, too many things. They document the offense, *spitting on patron*, and tack his picture on the wall of terrible sad losers, escort him out and release him into the afternoon. He stumbles into the sunshine.

Maybe if Kaia were here she would remind me that at the invisible level everything is the same, so you shouldn't mourn a little mucus from a stranger, that stranger is you, the mucus is you. Spitting on patron.

The Passenger

I AM SAILING ON no legs, passing as a car. The smeared lights are moving cat's eyes, blurry lightning bolts. Affectionate tickle on my arms, tingle of numbness in my deep throat, constant reminders of all the directions an evening could go, an infinite number, a twisting map. A top is spinning in the center of my pelvis, my genitals could consume this city. Cover the earth!

On the bus, well, I am too tall for this bus. I hold on to the slender silver pole, I rest my forehead against it. A woman is talking, saying, *stop scratching, stop scratching*. A room of typewriters chronicles every inner scroll. *I swear I feel him looking at the back of my head. If I don't like it, if I'm not comfortable, I'll just leave. I hate these pants. I need some new pants, seriously, that's my project for this weekend, new black pants*. Little black spots are scuttling around my feet, rats trying to hide from me, *me!* A member of your own family! Smile at it (*How do you make God laugh? Make a plan!*) and continue. The smell of urine getting stronger (*can't be far now*). A Chinese woman in a shiny outfit passes slowly. No barriers. My body is the sea. Drink air and breathe water. It's all good. It's all powdered diamonds. Everyone is getting off the bus but I prefer it here, everything I need.

Last stop! The voice of a preacher, a singer, a wave of overtones, shining like shells. . . .

Gotta turn in my coach up here, honey.

'Up here' is a sunken sea of dark buses, a grid of grimy metal surfaces, blocks wide.

Are you going home? I say.

Pretty soon, he says. *Pretty soon. Where you going?*

Right. Where? He shovels me back over softly, into the goofy, badly painted night, where inept aspiring crooks suck on shoplifted lollipops and the smiling sick sleep under the wheels of cars, whinnying in their dreams. Dust to dust. A patched-up pair of dolls sits on a ledge, swinging their legs in time, eating corn from cobs. I gather my orientation, swim toward Mission Street. I will find one of Maxxie's friends at Esta Noche if I don't find some other trouble, I'll find some skirt to hide in, not too tight, I will find something, or something will find me tonight, at least some pills to put my mind a little bit back together, or shush it.

THE MUSIC STOPS, CARS pull over, there is honking, the police descend quickly, sprinkling the land with their panicky flashes of red and blue, stretching ribbons of yellow tape. There he is. Nobody is smiling, even the weathered and leathered are shaking their heads in sad shock. A teenager, a boy, lies freshly dead in front of El Gigante burrito shop, the bottoms of his shoes bright white. His football jersey also white, hospital white. I know the boy is dead, everybody knows, even though there is no blood. No knife sticking out of his kidney. He is just certainly dead. And then there is the blood, a circle creeping darkly out from his head like a black halo.

A tattoo encircles his upper arm, a single delicate undulation of barbed wire. The sadness of this scene crushes me flat. That wasted body should have been alive. I fight to breathe through the weight of grief. Let's get out of here. Let's move to the next slide. Click. The next block down from the dead child, a woman's jeans reach up to the bottom of her ribs and are tied there with a rope, bagging her generous middle into two soft sacs. She wears a black leather vest, sits on a stool and smokes, bringing the cigarette to and from her mouth like an automated toy monkey. She's got blue eyeliner all the way around her eyes, her elbows on the bar. Behind the bar a joyful Nordic supermodel type woman with perfect skin is jiggling a cocktail shaker like a marimba, shaking it above each shoulder and shaking her butt along with it. I order a drink, a whiskey and coke, and they don't card me, and it ices my brain flat instantly and I'm thinking it will inject novocaine into my memory too please, but no I'm still seeing black blood creep out from under the dead boy, now forming a dark shining lake all around him, finally dripping over the shelf of the curb and running into the gutter like thick oil.

But maybe he is not dead after all. Perhaps it was a movie set, or a TV show. A school project. Smoke machines and purple lights all around him. He will resurrect and doves will land on his ears. His tattoo rubs off with alcohol. Maybe it's a Christian scare movie. Perhaps all the police were wearing fake uniforms. Perhaps if I had looked closely I would have seen that their badges said PHILADELPHIA or OZ or even were written in a pretend language because they were pretend cops. Maybe there were enormous lights and trailers and a director in a director's chair, and I just had been hypnotized by the drama in my gullible underslept psychedelic state and hadn't seen them. Perhaps I had not seen anything. Perhaps I had made it up, the white jersey, the beautiful arms, new shiny silver watch around his wrist. He lifts himself in a pushup and his face is the most beautiful angel. *I miss you everyday Sheila*, reads a scrawl on the paper towel box. *LaShay is La Gay. You da man. Where are you?*

Where are you?

EL GIGANTE IS CLOSED now and there is no sign of a child or a man or a person having died in front of it. There is not a candle or a flower or a balloon. There is not a chalk outline or a shred of yellow tape. There is nothing there except a giant sleeping potato man clutching a walkman. Oh, there it is, one piece of yellow tape, fluttering down the block.

I'M IN NORTH BEACH when the sun thinks about coming up. I follow a yawning girl walking to work, she unlocks the door to a café. I doze at a bus stop and soon the dawn breaks silver and the shop is opening and the city inhales and people with jobs are heading to work. The café girl flips the sign to APERTO! and I float in, the first customer. She makes a heart in the foam of my cappuccino. It costs two dollars, which is exactly what I have, and she gives me some 'free mistakes'—cookies from yesterday that they forgot to put the eggs in.

WHAT IF HIS MOTHER was driving down the street and happened upon the scene, found her child dead in a boil of police buzz and slavering onlookers?

What is the difference between you and your corpse?

Kaia used to ask that.

As an exercise.

Kaia I cannot answer it I cannot know it intellectually but I can occasionally taste it and smell it. Kaia it is a good question.

Goth

I TURN THE CORNER and there she is, angling her mirror so it shines in my eye, staring me down like a glowery gargoyle. She's crouched beside the wheel of a van, I'd have figured she was peeing but she is not. She snaps the mirror closed. Maxxie did not tell me she would be a child! Fourteen perhaps, gothic makeup sharpening tender features. Almond eyes, paper-thin white blouse.

What are you doing? I say.

I'm scraping rust off my ancient heart. Don't come closer, or I'll stab you in the chest with a piece of glass. Do you have the package?

Across the street, a mother struggles to get a stroller into the door of a massage parlor. Finally she gets it in.

I give the goth girl the package, she gives me an envelope of money. She's a kid, she runs off like a fairy. I can't do this.

Burnout

SPILLED INTO THE NIGHT again in my stupid bellhop whore costume. My golden epaulets are crusted with what I suspect is vomit from the last girl who wore it. The costumes are not washed often, but are they washed ever? Maxxie had insisted that I wear these new shiny red shoes he got me at Ross, they are sweet but they pinch and soon there are smiles of blood staining my white tights at the ankles.

I drink two Red Bulls and walk around and around at the biggest, most populated dance club but no one is buying any of the shit on my tray and my new wig feels crooked and smells like a Barbie, and most grievously they have just passed a law that you can't smoke in bars, so no one is buying my cigarettes or my ten-dollar cigars that I have at times sold for twenty or thirty dollars, and once, for one hundred, because people want to party.

Around four a.m., the speedfreak techno dancers will all want gum and lollipops, and for a brief spell I'll sell things fast like popcorn popping, but until then I am merely décor, and I prefer to sit in the VIP lounge and doze with a smile pasted to my face. A boy sits next to me and slowly gets closer, eventually his hand is under my ass massaging my butt, which is fine.

When I spill out of headquarters at dawn with my evening's wages barely in the double digits and my mouth dry and my blood sandy and wanting, I am sure that I will quit this gig and get a job. A job, like other people have. They'll pay me with a check, maybe I'll get a bank account and have a comfortable chair. Maybe I'll get a dog, or a pillow. Sensible shoes.

Enclosed

FENDI, WHO SEES WHORING as his best way of serving humanity, is certain that my next career move should be to become a peep show girl, not a stripper but really a dancer, how healing to connect with people like that, so raw and yet so protected. Also enclosed, literally, in a sisterhood. And if I am a lesbian or realize or decide that I am a lesbian, no problem, they're all lesbians. And it's also the best workout known to womankind. *You need to get in touch with your tralala, sister*, he'd said, touching my underchin with a shiny black fingernail, sending shivers down me and making me stand up straight. He even did a tarot card reading to prove it and grew ever more convinced. And that is how I find myself at Kinky Karole's on a Tuesday early evening, to just 'check it out.' First thing I see, after the front desk guy waves me through, is a line of black doors which must be the booths one enters to be the peepshow. Across from that is a small blonde woman in a glass cube, reclining on a satiny mini-bed, wearing a sheer red robe and enormous, red heart-shaped sunglasses, sucking a lollipop. The sign says her name's 'Desiree' but it's Anna Hosanna, I'm sure of it. My heart kicks. My heart stumbles. A tightly coiled pigtail against the front of her body. I want to squeeze her but there's glass.

Howdy stranger, she says, through a fuzzy intercom. *Come on up and see me sometime like right now. Shut the curtain.*

I enter the booth and shut the curtain and we have pseudo-privacy. She removes the sunglasses and there are her farmgirl eyes, crusted in white stardust. I stand still with my limbs clamped in so that I don't touch any ejaculate. The floor is sticky and the place smells like hot dick.

I knew our paths would cross, she says. *I heard you were here.*

She is untying the silky cords of her robe as she speaks.

San Diego wasn't the same without you, she says. *I missed you. Remember that time we snuck into the zoo? Haven't you missed me?*

She opens her robe and her breasts are there, but different, vulgar, fat purple orchids.

Do you like them? she says. *I just had them done.*

She bounces them in her flat palms, then presses them to the glass. She touches the glass with her tongue. This is a joke to her, but I don't want it, I want her body to be sacred, like it is. My queen! My queen in the harsh morning light, her crown crooked, her eyes shot. My queen, wiping the cum off her purse, counting the money. She peeks out to make sure there isn't a paying customer waiting. There's not. *Sorry*, she says. *Am I being hideous? I'm on speed and it makes me so gross and horny and CHATTY. It's good for this line of work. Don't say my real name please. I don't care but they care.*

AFTER BUGGY DIED EVERYONE got straight, she says. Everyone was becoming a boring junkie but now they're upstanding. Still boring. There are some funny stories though. I'll tell you sometime. Alexis is still strung out but everyone else is like in AA . . . well, not everyone but Dooney is, in and out like all the time and also kind of Christian. . . .

Buggy? Died? *Are you being serious?*

You didn't hear?, she says. *It was like six months ago.*

I haven't talked to anyone. I don't know anything. What happened?

Ooh, you went underground from the underground! He got that bacteria, from shooting up. He died fast. He looked bad, apparently his body was dark and full of holes. I'm sorry to tell you that.

Stop lying, I say, but she isn't, not about the important part, the dead part.

I SEE THE HOLES all over him, dark immediate and uniform like golf holes. Holes on his face. Holes where his eyes were.

I dig him up and he puts his oyster-cool arms around me like a baby.

Say goodbye.

In his hospital bed he expires limb by limb, each limb going limp and gray until it overcomes him with its melt. When only his head is left he is winding it around while mumbling divine phrases and then his own language then he slips off into total realization . . . he is packaged as dead so that we in this world can understand what happened. . . .

It wasn't the dirty needle, it was the windowsill sprouts, which evolved a special fungus to carry Buggy to the next world in its psychedelic wrapper . . . a carriage . . . Buggy, cross over!

Paid Friends

THE KITTENS LOUNGE BESIDE the tub as I bathe myself. They lounge like paid-by-the-hour-whores who've been paid for a whole day in advance and just want to relax and be beautiful and try not to eat too much. I am afraid they could get in the water and drown. I supervise them very well. One big gray baby slips into the water and stays there, calm. I pull and push her out, she isn't mad. Another group of furry gray kittens falls in, they don't fight the water, they nestle down in it, they relax. I pull them out, their bodies heave a little with coughs. Every one of them wants to be alive.

Invisibles

THE BEACH HERE IS very different from what I'm used to. It's never warm, for one. Under rocks live secret, outdated families. Their RVs disappear like vampires when the sun approaches, but during the night they are there, the children in muslin bonnets, a girl looking out from a window then disappearing, leaving only a swinging curtain. They are there. Silent ghostly cousins, transient, undocumented half-visibles. Playing with dolls from the seventies, another sort of lost.

A barge is floating silent and effortless, under one bridge, under another bridge, as if a part of nature. As if it thinks it is. The life span of a machine. Buggy is out there in the freezing water but loving it, he's wearing tighty whities and his hair is longer now, his face is turned toward the sky and he's grimacing happily, he's got some muscles. A man is throwing a tennis ball and his dog is fetching it. His dog leaps into the water and swims and gets it.

A collection of haggard crows visits, malnourished, sinking in low circles. They are made from cheap brassieres, scratchy polyester lace, all tangled up, feathers tacky. They fly in close to my head, my ears, wanting to eat my eyeballs, my nipples, to pierce my lips, to draw beads of blood. They are looking at me through gluey crossed eyes, frowning, going lower and lower, I know they can kill me and they want to. Despite their feeble appearance they are possessed by bloodlust, and I am a swollen cherry of heavy, rich blood, I am nutrition for them. This again. I need to get out of here!

Also I am not going to be a stripper. I won't pretend that far.

Brûlée

I KNOW! I WILL be a cook.

This is how you use the gun. Don't use the gun unless someone orders the crème brûlée. Am I perfectly clar-o? Do not use the gun to have fun.

I want fun! On the street I melt their clothes off with my silver crème brûlée gun. The nakeds hover and shake, hiding their faces in their elbows. *Poor me*, they think, banned from Eden.

HER TITTIES BOB IN front of me like two grapefruits knocking slowly together. If they made a sound it would have been a low gong. I am magnetized in.

Anna's black eyeliner comes to darling uptick at the edge of her eyelids. She twirls a red feather around her scarred nipple—scarred, but so precise and tidy—and looks up at me, vamping. Those are her pearly lips and that is her sweet skin. But I don't have a feeling for her now. I'm like a movie camera, dollying slowly backwards. And there is a man outside, waiting to enter and shoot his semen against the glass. Plexiglass.

Everything is changing all the time!

Anna/Desiree does not work here anymore. We don't know where she is. We couldn't tell you if we did know. For privacy reasons obviously. But anyway we don't.

Angels

MAXXIE MADE LA SOUND good, I could work for famous people just as kind of a paid friend, he knows tons of famous people, he is well loved, he is *bien connu*, and it's totally fun and weird there, there's glitter in the sidewalks, ladies have surgery on their assholes to make them look tighter and younger and pinker, everyone is fucking their trainer. I mean there's so much entertainment, plus the beauty, it's like nature versus civilization in one long, slow, sun-drunk battle that nature is destined to win. Maxxie is going to drive me in his silver Mercedes and help me get set up with some nice cush work and see some old friends. We'll soak in their hot tub, I can sleep in the same bed where so-and-so did so-and-so to so-and-so who is so-and-so's daughter, but not by blood. It sounds fun and weird and I am ready for this next thing, working at a restaurant fucking sucks and anyway I got fired. My boss let me down easy, he told me I was 'a dreamer.' In LA I will come into bloom under an arc of bougainvillea, manually squeezing oranges into juice in the sun until my biceps are defined like creamy ropes. I will be warm and sea-salted but still far enough away from the crime scene of my younger years to escape the magnetism of disabling and boring tragedies. I'll live on leaves I find popping out of the sidewalks. I will smell of sweet soap. I will 'celebrate my 21st,' as Maxxie puts it, floating in a neon claw in a sweet aquamarine pool, surrounded by faux rocks and sipping kale juice from a biodegradable straw while lithe girls do swandives to bring me more ice cubes. I'll be a dreamer.

I'm going to go! I say.

Jubilant, we bring our first armful of things out to the car. Only it's not there. Maxxie remembers he parked it on Sutter Street actually or no it was Bush then Pine and then there, and we are walking up and down the hills carrying two suitcases apiece (all his) plus Fluffer, crashing through tourists, it's not here nor there. Finally he thinks it must have been towed. He convinces the pizza man to let him use the phone and is screaming at City Tow, *This is unlawful! This is America!*

They didn't steal it, Fendi says flatly when we return to the apartment with cashed-out hearts and sunburnt noses. *It was repossessed.*

Maxxie is so dejected that he cannot speak, and can only nurse a bottle of pills he found in the knife drawer. He sleeps clutching the empty bottle, topless, wagging the biggest pill bottle I've ever seen.

Freeway

DESPITE MAXXIE BEING TERRIBLY sad, the kind of sad that lies over the body like a poisonous mist, despite the attendant dark mood that has settled over our whole cluster, I have a bell ringing inside me, deep and private, that heralds happiness ahead, a feeling that I will punch out into the world, LA will be the next stop but the feeling is not specific to LA. It is the feeling of the decision to live, it is fancy shopping bags knocking together inside me. Maybe this is how normal people feel when they go 'off to college.' I make lemon water and sacred minerals to cure everyone's mini-ennui and then I clean the floor very well with the lemon water, slowly and precisely I wipe with this old t-shirt until I've lifted layers of life and death from the linoleum and the room smells new and Maxxie is stirring in a way that suggests that he might get up—one stout velour leg lifts into the air and the toes flex—and Fluffer contributes a soft, long fart—now back to napping.

The sun outside is certain, the curtain is lifted by a little wind, the smell of the outside is uncommonly pleasant and sweet, maybe someone is chopping basil or making coconut rice. Next stop coconut rice. I have been incubated inside a warm egg, I feel perfectly seasoned by death and drag queens, perfectly buttoned. My heart makes a shape around my dead friend, my friend who I will not see again. No matter what happens I will not see him again. And my heart is cracked—sometimes it feels like a little axe stuck right in the center of it, just hanging—say it isn't so, say not *him*, that little creature, my impossibly talented little booger-licking freak—I also feel put into relief by it. He is dead and I am not. I am here. And I want to be here for a while. I want wholesome things, the coconut rice, cotton socks, to feel the sun drench my bones and the bones set heavy into the earth . . . to feel the miles zipping underneath me miraculously as I rocket off to something totally unforeseen . . . in a diamond-colored Mercedes would have been great but we'll get there, if we're destined to get there we'll get there . . . America!

Fendi's been wearing the same turquoise sequined dress, including while sleeping, for more than a week. As she puts blonde extensions in my hair, the time marked by sighs, I can smell her, I can feel her heat, and I feel a little strange, a little faint. Tomorrow, tomorrow is the day that I will rise before dawn, leave my note of goodbye on the coffee table, take my bags and slowly back out of the apartment, never to return. Her long nails are clicking in a calypso rhythm—how does she get any work done with those things on? How DOES she do it, as they say? When I begin to hear something.

It began like a deep growl, a dark primal warning. I thought it was a personal experience I was having, then I thought it must be Fluffer, then I felt a pulsing in my leg and Fendi grabbed me to her body, her sequins were hard and pressed into my skin brutally and I cried out. *Get away from the window you fucker!* She called me a fucker! She was strong. I was a babe in her arms as the window, on cue, curved inward then burst, sending glass like rain, then the bookshelf came down, then the rack of dresses. Pill bottles and abalone shells went careening through the air. Fendi pulled me to the front door, she squeezed my head to her chest, her knifey nails against my ears. *My kidney stoooooone!*, Maxxie cried as that and everything else that was on the coffee table—ribbons of platinum hair, peanut shells, bits of foil, scratched-off lottery tickets, the dust from the scratches of those tickets—flew off and crashed down and bounced and we heard the sounds of bursting glass from near and far, big and small, a symphony of destruction, and cars crashing, and car alarms jolting to life, and ladies screaming, and men yelling, do this and *don't* do that, and things hitting the ground and then scraping. Stuff cracking, maybe trees, maybe telephone poles. Fluffer's metal dinner dish bouncing like a tennis ball then spinning on its lip, the dress rack sliding back and forth, dress arms and unitards waving in panic, angels and blackbirds and desks and boots and rice grains and hamburgers zipping like shooting stars through the open window. An American flag sails in from the outside, nearly landing on Maxxie, who's grabbed Fluffer, and everyone is looking around at everyone like *is it over yet?*

WHEN THE SHAKING STOPS we look around to see who is dead or bleeding or hurt and everyone is okay and doing the same grim scan. There is an unnatural silence, the world has lurched to a stop. My hand over my heart and it's still beating. I take my envelope of money, I remove glass shards from the tongues of my sneakers and put them on slowly, I right the dress rack that had fallen over and was blocking the front door, nudge Fluffer's overturned dish . . . no, the world will not be okay, and I won't, and Maxxie won't, and no one will be okay, and yes, this is the moment when I will fling myself into it. Just because something's futile doesn't mean it's hopeless. My legs work so well as I sail down the stairs into the devastated perfect afternoon.

Acknowledgments

For their support in the creation of this work the author would like to thank:

Radar Productions and Ragdale Foundation, The Exploratorium, Bruce Benderson, Camille Roy, Samara Halperin, Adrienne Heloise, Desiree Holman, Zoey Kroll, Lena Lucille, Bobby Ray, Sarah Reiwitch, the Washburns, Erin Wilson, Krista and Gil Cabrera, Nadine Felix, Fernando Felix, Tom and Sondra, Michelle Tea, publisher and editor Elaine Katzenberger, publicist Jolene Torr and everyone else at City Lights, and the friends who incited this work.